The Secret Garden

Kingston Library

H ERE is an excellent opportunity of acquiring a fine series of books at a reasonable price. Well-presented stories with themes of wide popular interest make up the Kingston Library. All the stories chosen for inclusion have one quality in common—they make excellent reading.

List of Titles

BIGGLES, PIONEER AIR FIGHTER	by	Capt. W. E. Johns
BIGGLES OF THE CAMEL SQUADRON	,,	Capt. W. E. Johns
BIGGLES in THE CRUISE OF THE CONDOR	,,	Capt. W. E. Johns
BIGGLES and THE BLACK PERIL	,,	Capt. W. E. Johns
BIGGLES FLIES AGAIN	,,	Capt. W. E. Johns
BIGGLES OF THE SPECIAL AIR POLICE	,,	Capt. W. E. Johns
BIGGLES OF 266	,,	Capt. W. E. Johns
SON OF BLACK BEAUTY	,,	Phyllis Briggs
THE SECRET GARDEN	,,	Phyllis Briggs
DEBORAH'S SECRET QUEST	,,	Cecilia Falcon
ELIZABETH'S GREEN WAY	,,	Jean Vaughan
THE LITTLE COUNTESS	,,	Frances Cowen
THE ADVENTURES OF TOM SAWYER	,,	Mark Twain
THE ADVENTURES OF HUCKLEBERRY FINN	,,	Mark Twain
YARNS OF BLUE WATER	,,	Douglas V. Duff
THE RUSES OF RUBY-ANNE	,,	Douglas V. Duff
KING SOLOMON'S MINES	,,	H. Rider Haggard
QUEEN SHEBA'S RING	,,	H. Rider Haggard
NADA THE LILY	,,	H. Rider Haggard
DAVID COPPERFIELD	,,	Charles Dickens

The
SECRET GARDEN

PHYLLIS BRIGGS

Kingston
Library

THE THAMES PUBLISHING CO,
LONDON

MADE AND PRINTED IN GREAT BRITAIN BY PURNELL AND SONS, LTD.
PAULTON (SOMERSET) AND LONDON

CONTENTS

CHAPTER I

ENTER MARCUS

THE telephone shrilled in the hall of Bramble Cottage, and Merryl raced to answer it.

"Oh, is that you, Teddy?" she exclaimed—with pleasure, because it was nice that the 'gang', as they called themselves, had taken to her and made her one of themselves ever since that day three months ago when she had come to live with her aunt at Flaxstead.

"Yes, it's me," a boyish voice replied pleasantly if ungrammatically. "Doing anything particular this afternoon?"

"No," the girl acknowledged with a little smile. "Why?"

As she stood there with the receiver to her ear, her head aslant, the sun lit up little glowing sparkles on her corn-coloured hair. Her dark-blue eyes gazed out at the glorious summer landscape, so different from what she had always known. Far off, shivering warmly in the heat, were the purple moors and the heights of Dillbury Beacon. Right under the hall-window was Aunt Penny's cottage garden, warm and scented, and between these two

7

points stretched all the lovely rolling wooded country in which Great and Little Flaxstead nestled.

"That's great!" Teddy went on. "'Member me telling you of that Dog and Pet Show next month? It's rather a big thing here, and old Sir What's-'is-name gave a cup about ten years ago to be competed for each year and held by the winner one year!"

"Yes——?" Merryl wrinkled her brow.

"We won it last year with our Roy of Connisdale. Cup's got to go back now—that's the rule—to be competed for again. You said you'd like to see it, so if you like to pop over on your bike I'll get it out of the safe when Dad's out."

"That would be fun—rather!" she answered warmly. "I will! It must be fun winning cups with dogs!"

She could not help wishing that Aunt Penny had a dog, but there never had been a dog at Bramble Cottage, Teddy had told her. Not that Miss Penny disliked them; she was rather fond of animals; but she had 'never got round to having one', he had said.

Merryl fetched her bike from the toolshed, propped it against the gate, and pumped up both tyres good and hard. These stony country-lanes were not so easy to ride along as the city streets; but there were compensations. Here you might see a lark drop out of the blue after spilling down a cascade of song, then run on twinkling feet through the knotty grass stems to its secret nest; or sometimes a stoat would flash over the path, or a blackbird spring up clacking indignantly from the poppied tangle of hedgerow grass.

"It's a gorgeous day," she breathed as she cycled along the little lanes leading to the main Flaxstead road.

The soft hot wind whipped gold tendrils into her eyes. She slowed as she neared the road, because she could hear the banging and thundering of a big lorry coming. Just as she reached the end of the road and came out into a pool of sunshine the vehicle came abreast and roared past in a flurry of yellow dust. It was going in the same direction that Merryl must take, so she swung along after it.

"That looks frightfully unsafe," she thought as she noted a crate, the hindermost one of the lorry's load, which had bumped its way to the very edge and now overhung it by six inches. Merryl bent forward, pedalling her fastest, but she knew she could not catch up.

"Hi, driver, hi, you!" she yelled with all the power of her lungs, but the man in the lorry's cabin had his ears so filled with the sounds of his own tumultuous progress that he could not hear her.

"Hi, your crate!" Merryl screamed as the lorry went over another bump in the road.

The crate bounced happily and now teetered on the very edge. One more lurch and it would be off.

In spite of furious riding, Merryl was dropping far behind, and she reflected ruefully that there was just nothing she could do about the matter. It was as well for herself that she was not just behind the lorry, for ten seconds later the inevitable happened. The lorry took one final spring into the air over an unexpected stone and the crate flew off to land with a splitting crash in the road, where it lay while feeble little dust-clouds eddied about it.

Merryl braked and swerved all in one movement, and in her efforts not to run smack into the wreckage came off in the road. Much shaken, she picked herself up and with trembling hands brushed the dust off her frock.

"Well," she thought grimly, "at this rate I shall be some time getting to Teddy's. I shall have to stop and drag all that smash out of the fairway. Oh, bother it; I ought to have taken the lorry's number! Well, that's just too bad."

She went across to the crate and got the shock of her life, for a small head with liquid dark eyes and melancholy expression was thrusting itself through the broken sides. It was a baby ape, but it looked just like a small doll with reddish brown hair and a domed upper lip, which puckered petulantly as it whimpered softly.

"You poor little scrap!" she cried, and went down on her knees by the crate.

Instantly, two hairy little arms were held out appealing. She wrenched the broken laths apart and pulled the ape out. It cuddled up to her, sliding its long arms round her neck and holding up its queer flat lips for a kiss.

"Oh, what a shame to drive like that and give you such a shock!" Merryl cried, stroking the ape's little bullet-head. "Well, now I expect I'd better take you home till I find out where you belong."

She puzzled as to how she was going to manage. Finally she sat the ape in her bicycle-basket and was going to mount when she discovered that her rear tyre was flat, for in her fall the machine had struck the bank and a piece of jutting barbed-wire had pierced the tyre.

That settled it. She would have to walk back.

"Good thing I hadn't got any farther," she thought philosophically, but even then she was amazed at the differing assessment one makes of distance when awheel and afoot.

It was past four when she got back, and Aunt Penny was working in the front garden spraying the ramblers and looking down the lane from time to time.

"Tea's ready," she exclaimed in her gentle brisk way. "Goodness, what on earth have you got there?"

"It's a baby ape," Merryl answered, disentangling the creature from its basket, to which it clung in frenzied fear of being snatched from something which even in so short a time it had come to know was safe and comfy.

"Let go, silly. Auntie, can you undo his fingers?"

"I'm—I'm not sure whether I quite dare touch him, dear." Her aunt hesitated, but the ape turned its imploring face to her and she melted.

"Come indoors and I'll see if I can find it something to eat. Where *did* you get it?"

Aunt Penny listened and nodded and clicked her tongue and wondered how people could drive so recklessly all the time Merryl was telling her.

"And you're sure you didn't hurt yourself?"

"Oh, I'm okay," the girl answered cheerfully as she peeled an orange for the ape. "Of course, I don't know if it's what he ought to be getting, but he likes it already. What shall we call him? He'll have to have a name, even if it's only for a day or two."

"You could call him Marcus," her aunt suggested as she filled an old clothes-basket with straw to make the ape a bed. "Your uncle out in Uganda had a pet ape he called that."

Marcus eyed her preparations with eager delight in his button eyes. His top lip lifted and he wrinkled his brows so that his sad, wise countenance was absurdly comical.

"Okay, he's Marcus," Merryl said, and she went outside to mend her bike.

When she was through with this it was nearly seven and the westering sun was sliding down behind the church elms. With a feeling that she had somehow let Teddy down, she went in to find the telephone ringing fussily on its stand.

"I expect that's Teddy," she thought, and Teddy it certainly was.

"Oh, Merry, is that you? You weren't quite so thrilled as you made out to be, then!"

"I wasn't pretending. I was thrilled to come and see the cup, only, you see——"

"It wasn't worth bothering so far," Teddy went on in a peevish tone. "I shan't be in such a hurry to ask you again."

"You needn't," Merryl cried, her own temper rising, but there was a wicked gleam in her eyes. "You see, I met Marcus, and he was so sweet I took him home to tea at Aunt's!"

There was a stunned silence. And then: "Who is Marcus?" Teddy asked sharply. "He must be a new boy here. He'd better mind what he's about, shoving his beastly nose in where he isn't wanted. Well, look, Merryl, can you come tomorrow?"

She could have choked with laughter at the change in his tone.

"Yes, of course I will, and can I bring Marcus to see you?"

"If you must," Teddy said grudgingly, "but if he don't behave I'll shove his face in."

She rang off and went to help Aunt Penny in the kitchen. It was anything but a restful night. Who, Merryl reflected, would keep a zoo? It was the third time she had got up in answer to Marcus's miserable whining, and she would have been amazed if she could have seen the future and how strange her own words would someday seem to her.

But when day came at last, the baby ape seemed to have quite recovered his spirits Merryl spent an hour phoning round to find some trace of his owners or the driver of the lorry, but without any success.

"We'll have to put a bit in the local rag about him," she said as she warmed him some porridge. He was sitting on Miss Penny's lap, watching and grunting contentedly, and Merryl paused. "I've a good mind to enter him for a show as a pet, if he's still here next month," she chuckled.

But Marcus was not interested, for he kept picking titbits from the plates and pushing them between his rubbery lips with a speed of action and determination that were very noteworthy.

"No, not *that*!" Merryl had to scold him as she brought his breakfast, for the ape was now reaching for the silver coffee-pot, charmed by his own reflection in it. They took it away from him, and also the sugar basin, and then of course he was furious and screamed.

"I'll take him over to Teddy's and give you some peace," the girl said, and they set off.

But she had seen enough of him by now to know that if he were annoyed he might be difficult to handle, so she got an old leather belt and with a little contriving buckled part of it round the ape's waist and kept the other end in her hand. They went on foot, Marcus ambling by her side in a funny squat-legged shuffle, peering up into her face and squeaking, grunting and chattering away.

It was all of four miles to Teddy's, and long before that place was reached Marcus had definitely had enough. He sat down in the road, waved his long hairy arms over his head, and hooded his brows over his liquid eyes. He refused to move another step.

"Baby!" Merryl chided him, but sarcasm was of no more use than coaxing and at last she had to pick him up and start off across some open fields in what seemed like a short cut.

The ape was quite heavy. He whimpered his gratitude so sweetly that she reflected that if she traced his owners it was going to be quite a wrench parting from him. He seemed to understand what she said to him, and he had shown many times that morning that he would come to her when he would not stir for poor well-meaning Aunt Penny.

After getting over one or two gates the two came to another main road and the workings where a new bridge was being built across the valley so as to do away with a dangerous level-crossing on another route. An arch of graceful, openwork steel already spanned the valley, and the men working on it looked like flies. The sounds of riveting came as a faint chattering sound.

Merryl turned away hastily to pass this object, at which Marcus was gazing longingly, for the airy contraption had no terrors for him; his ancestors had swung at far greater heights as they made their way through jungle depths.

Across the next field they came in sight of Teddy's, where the gang lived. He was out in the farmyard adjoining the house and was watching out for her, evidently with gloomy curiosity.

"Where is Marcus?" he yelled when they were within earshot. "*What?* That comical brute?" The boy's face turned a fine purple scarlet as he realised that she was laughing at him. "You just wait till I get him by himself," he muttered, casting a venomous glance at the poor ape. But as she approached, his curiosity got the better of him and he allowed that Marcus might have his points.

"I say!" he shouted. "Here, Dodie, Ken! Come and look what Merry's brought with her. She's starting a zoo at Bramble Cottage."

The girl was staring at him as the other members of the gang came running.

"Do you know—you've given me an idea," she said softly.

"Are you really going to keep him?" Dodie asked enviously, for even a farmful of animals was not enough for her.

"Hope so—isn't he cute?" Merryl said.

Ken begged for the privilege of leading Marcus round the yard on his leather lead, and as they all wanted to play with him at once the ape was in a fair way to being spoilt. His spirits rose and he began to show off, dancing up and down in his peculiar four-legged way, 'arms' bent, legs bowed. He scowled and coughed, he put out his lips as if about to spit, and he screamed in their faces.

They were in fits of laughter, but he took that in good part and danced all the more wildly. Then, just when no one was expecting it, Marcus snatched the leather strap out of Ken's hands and holding it high as if it were a train and he were a fine lady afraid of falling over it dashed across the yard and into the house.

There was a scream and crash as Mary the maid, who was clearing out the lunch things, met him in the hall.

"Come back!" Merryl called to him, but she was so weak and breathless with laughing that she could only squeak.

They cornered the ape finally under the grand piano, and Dodie took charge of him.

"Look, Merry," Teddy said when they could speak again, "Dad's gone out now, so if you come I'll show you the cup." He took her into Mr. Carter's study. He did not mention the fact that he was not supposed to touch the safe or get the cup out of it. There was an expression of pride and delight on his face as he opened the safe and showed her how it worked.

"Dad doesn't know I know," he boasted, "but I've watched him heaps of times. There, what do you think of it?"

"Why, it's marvellous!" Merryl cried, and the cup really was worth seeing. It was not very large, standing only about eight inches high, but it was hand-carved and there were semi-precious stones worked into the design. Its surface was a glittering mass of scrolls, flowers and fruit. It had a hinged cover and stood on sturdy ball feet.

"Now you'd better put it back," Merryl said uneasily. "Thanks for showing me."

"Oh, it's all right," Teddy said airily. "There's a bit about it, a cutting in the paper about last year's Show, and Dad kept it. I'll read it to you."

"Don't," Merryl urged, for she thought it wasn't quite the thing for Teddy to be rummaging about on his father's desk among his private papers.

But the boy had pounced on the cutting. "Listen," he was beginning, when there was a crash and a scream from the girl. She had turned just in time to see the ape go tearing out of the room waving over his head the prize cup. Thinking over it long afterwards, she came to the conclusion that he had seen in it a likeness to the coffee-pot he had so coveted at breakfast. But now the pressing need was to catch him and take his treasure from him before he could do it any damage. She shuddered as she heard it clang as Marcus caught the door a thwack with it in passing.

"Dodie, help! Ken, quick!" she cried as she raced along.

Teddy, stricken with unhappy fears, thundered at her heels. If only the wretched ape would make for his favourite nook under the piano again they had him! Unfortunately, Ken, hearing cries for help, burst out from a side room, followed by Dodie. They had taken their eyes off Marcus for only one moment, but he had watched his chance and that was enough time for him.

Seeing them ahead now made him turn to the left. He saw an open door and darted into the orchard. His comical three-legged gambolling as he carried the cup high, and the speed at which he could move, would have made them all laugh again if the situation had not been so serious. He waved the prize cup round and round his bullet-head.

"Head him off, Teddy," Dodie cried helplessly, but to head anything off you must get in front of it and no one could do that.

They raced round the orchard, and Marcus had sufficient sense to keep out of the trees, for they were too far apart and he seemed to know that if they treed him he was done. It seemed so easy in theory to catch him. Time and again they thought they had done it. One of them attracted his attention while another crept up behind him, but always his acute hearing saved him just in time. They thought that things could not very well be worse, for already Marcus had dashed the cup against the ground several times in his baffled petulance, as if he would defy them.

But even light-hearted Ken went white to the lips when Marcus, seeing his chance, went up the orchard wall like a flash of light. One moment he stood atop capering joyously, outlined against the dazzle of the summer sky, jabbering at them. The next and he had swooped from their sight.

"The bridge!" Merryl's eyes were wide with horror. "He saw it and wanted to go out along it when we were coming. He's remembered!"

She was right. Marcus had remembered the bridge just as he had remembered the coffee-pot. He had known that both were forbidden to him, and with all an animal's deep cunning he had bided his time. The prize cup had brought them both to mind.

Merryl ran as she had never run in her life before across those sunny fields. The day had turned furiously hot, and she felt giddy with fear of what her new charge might do. Was she gaining even the least little bit on that black wretch flying along before her? She had been first to the gate in the wall and so was ahead of the others.

But Teddy, who was very nearly a champion runner, was catching her up. Doggedly she was planning what they must do. They must shout to the workmen as soon as they were near enough and ask them to head the little brute off. Would she have enough breath left with which to shout?

There was the bridge. Now! She looked, but to her dismay saw no one working. It was Saturday afternoon now, and the men had all packed up and gone. Their tool-hut was locked and deserted. No one could stop the ape now. With a scream of triumph he ran out nimbly on the spidery erection, which to him was a secure and safe road. Not till he was halfway did the ape pause, and then it was to squat down on the girders as if suddenly tired and begin to hammer dolefully at the steelwork with the ball feet of the prize cup.

Teddy reached the bridgehead at the same time as Merryl. A black scowl was distorting the boy's good-looking face and he pushed the girl to one side.

"This is no place for you. I'll get him, Merry," he ordered, though the journey ahead might have daunted tougher nerves than his. But she caught at his arm.

"No; no, can't you see, I'll have to do it? He doesn't like you! He spat at you twice in the house and tried to bite you when you hauled him from under the piano. If you go he'll just move on ahead and we shall lose him and the cup. Or he might chuck it down on the railway lines and then we'll be done!"

"Yes," cried Dodie, who had run up in time to hear. She flung herself upon the furious Teddy. "Ken, help me. No one must go out there—no—not even you, Merry!"

"Well, I'm going," Merryl cried stormily and started before they could stop her.

It was not so bad at first, for much of the steel framework was filled in, but soon she came to the open part and then she wished she had not been so bold. But she would not go back.

"Marcus, Marcus!" she called to him as she scrambled forward. There was just the chance that he would hear and heed and come to her, bringing his trophy with him. On knees that were trembling with the effort she was making not to slip, the girl toiled on, while the gang watched helplessly, raging that they could not follow and help her.

Between the gaping openings in the steel structure, Merryl could see the railway lines gleaming far below. As she crept on she was praying that no train might pass thundering on its way north. Undoubtedly the noise and clouds of billowing steam would scare the last wits out of the miserable Marcus and he would drop the cup before running screaming and whimpering back to her for comfort.

Now the girl was on her hands and knees, for as she got further out she dared not walk upright any longer. She seemed to sway, or else it was the bridge swaying and shaking with her movements. Something seemed to be wanting to pull her over the edge. Only fifty feet to go. Marcus was sitting watching her moodily; his little joke seemed to have lost its relish. She began to call again softly, her voice shaking. He shifted uneasily and went on staring at her, his dark eyes so liquid that it looked as if he were shedding tears of rage or despair.

"You come on now," she cried and could have shouted for joy as he began to move towards her slowly. Only fifteen feet apart now; and then far off the whistle of an express shrilled.

"Marcus, come quickly!" she wailed.

He came, but, oh, so slowly, with tired shufflings and haltings!

"Ah!" she cried as she reached him and caught him by the leather belt, all frayed to tassels at the end. It was still a help to hold him by. He was only a youngster, and dog-tired with all his adventures. All the wickedness had oozed out of him for the time being. Not till she had the cup in the other hand did Merryl breathe freely again, and even then there was the return journey. She could see the faces of the three watchers, and they waved encouragement at her. But tears of relief were dimming her eyes.

Marcus, subdued and trembling, pressed against her side and made walking worse than it was when she had been alone, for now, what with holding him and the cup, she must stay upright. How she got back she was never quite sure. But she reached the bridgehead just as the express thundered through and the ape flung himself upon her with a yell of fear and buried his face in her frock.

They made their way back and put the cup in the safe again and no one said very much. Then Teddy gave vent to his feelings.

"If you can't find that brute's people, you'll have to send him to a zoo," he said. "He'll drive us crackers else."

"Yes, he shall go into a zoo," the girl answered, with an odd smile. "I'll tell you all about it another time, but now I'd better hurry back. Marcus is tuckered out!"

"And what about us?" the boy asked hotly, but she laughed and ran.

CHAPTER 2

THE SECRET GARDEN

"I THINK that is a stunning idea!" Teddy said. "A zoo! Now, why did *we* never think of that?"

The gang were all sitting round a little table in Granny Gubbins's garden, where Merryl had proposed a meeting. They used Granny Gubbins's quite a lot as her tea-house-cum-petrol-station was halfway between Carter's Farm and Bramble Cottage.

Two bottles of ginger-pop and four glasses stood on the table, and wasps were crawling round the wet circles of sweetness left by the bottles where they had fizzed over.

"A zoo!" Dodie cried ecstatically. "It's wizard, it's super! But where are we to get the animals from? We've only got one ape, and he may have to go back when we've traced his folk."

"Well, I thought it would be fun to plan," Merryl said, "and we'll do it all frightfully real and have a president and rules and fellows!"

"What fellows?" Teddy cried indignantly, his good-looking face darkening.

"Don't be a goose," Merryl cried impatiently.

"And it ought to be *gander*," Ken whispered to Dodie, his eyes twinkling wickedly.

"A fellow is the fancy name they give to zoo members," Merryl explained.

"Oh," Teddy grunted. "Soppy sort of lay-out, but if that's the rules——! Who's going to be president?" he went on hopefully.

"I am," Merryl answered calmly. "It was my idea as a stunt, but you can be treasurer and secretary, Teddy; you're such a live wire on figures!"

"Okay," the treasurer said, somewhat mollified.

They discussed the fascinating new game at length.

"Accommodation and running expenses are the snag," Teddy said, for he had heard Mr. Carter going on about bills for cattle-food and poultry-meal.

Dodie rubbed her nose reflectively. "Accommodation? There's no room at the farm, that *is* certain, and, anyway, it wants to be posher than that. What about Bramble Cottage, Merryl? Does that field at the back belong to your aunt?"

" 'Fraid not; wish it did. But, anyway, we'll have to go slow as we've nothing but Marcus as yet."

"Are you young people done?" Granny Gubbins asked from the doorway. "There's a car-party coming at twelve, so if you can skip it I'll wipe down my tables."

So the first board-meeting of the Flaxstead Private Zoo broke up.

Merryl hurried home to take the ape for a run, for she felt conscience-stricken when she left poor Aunt Penny to cope alone. As she neared Bramble Cottage, a presentiment of trouble came to her. Everything was very quiet and there was no one out in the front garden. In the little living-room was evidence of a struggle.

"Oh, I oughtn't to have left her to give him his breakfast," Merryl thought, and raced upstairs, for the sight of a broken plate, porridge adhering lumpily to the tablecloth, and a broken pane of glass, were disturbing.

"Aunt Penny?" she called anxiously.

"Oh, is that you, dear? I am glad you're back. I simply dare not leave this cupboard door. I've got him inside and I had to stand guard over it. He was in one of his unreasonable moods and he wouldn't eat his breakfast. I was as patient as Job, but finally I had to spank him with my hair-brush and then of course he went clean crazy, so I shut him up!"

"How awful," Merryl choked. "I *am* so sorry. I'll take him out for his run now!"

With a sigh of relief, Miss Penny went downstairs to get on with her morning chores, and Merryl cautiously opened the cupboard door. At first she could see nothing inside, and then from the far corner two luminous eyes glowed beseechingly up into hers and the ape began to whimper like a child afraid of the dark.

"Oh, darling!" she crooned to him, and he stumbled forward, put his arms round her neck and buried his face against her shoulder, while funny little tremors like sobs shook him.

"There, there, it's all right. You're not going to be bad any more now, are you? We'll go walkies!"

Marcus felt himself tenderly where he could still sense the humiliating sting of the hairbrush. She got him downstairs and out into the lane as quickly as possible, for she felt that Miss Penny had been provoked enough.

The morning was promising. No rain had fallen for several days and the only clouds were lacy little affairs which the morning had drawn across the far horizon. The voices of farmhands from fields where the generous hay was being cut sounded near at hand, and sharp, as if some unseen wave were carrying them. The hot sun drew spicy scents from the hedgerows, where the pale faces of the dog-roses were lifted to gaze skywards.

Marcus bounded up and down on his bent legs and waved his long hairy arms about. Every so often he would pause, throw one arm over his own shoulder, long black hand extended, fingers hooked, and give his back a satisfying scratch. He had quite got over his misery. Love and pleasure shone in his expressive eyes. Merryl felt a warm glow of pity for the poor little waif, and a hope—not indulged for the first time—that no trace of his owners would ever turn up.

They had reached the end of the lane when she felt a gentle tug. Marcus had the end of his leathern lead in his hand and was pulling it fretfully in the hope of a little run in freedom. She glanced swiftly up and down the lane. All was quiet with the brooding hush of a coming hot day.

"Okay!" She slipped off the lead, and the ape flapped his rubbery lips together in an appreciative way, grinning and dancing. All along on their right was a high, ten-foot wall over which trees leaned, their trunks out of sight. Merryl had noticed this wall before and wondered what was behind it, for there was no gate nor door all down this stretch of it. There was something forbidding in the hard bricks, which offered no foot or hand hold, so close together did they lie. Mystery hung over what lay on the far side.

Somewhere a car honked and a big roadster appeared purring along on noiseless wheels, its bulk almost spanning the lane. Marcus gave one bound into the air to show his disapproval. He disliked porridge and hairbrushes, but more than all he disliked cars, having painful remembrances of a certain lorry-ride in which he had been slung about miserably in his crate.

B

Merryl had not time to grasp at his lead again or snap the catch-hook into position, but she knew he was not run over, for he had taken one flying leap over the dry ditch into the stinging-nettles and lady's bedstraw. The big car brushed past and was gone in a flash, and so was Marcus!

"Where are you? Come here!" Merryl cried. She could not believe her eyes. Things like this happened on the stage in London, yes, but they were tricks, carefully prepared. Here there was no trick. The ape had simply vanished. Every bit of him was gone, his voice as well. A few moments ago he had been chattering and chuckling, coughing now and again in the silly little way he had, and now nothing but perfect silence reigned. A thrush on a high bough sang: "Give it up, give it up!"

"Marcus!" Merryl implored, casting a look of dislike at the maddening bird. She caught up a big stick out of the hedge and began probing at the lush growth. "Hello! What's this?" Her stick had disappeared suddenly into emptiness. She pulled away masses of thick grass hanging in a matted veil and there was a large round hole. The sunshine gleamed a few inches into its grim mouth and after that was blackness. It was, however, dry.

"A drain under the wall," she thought, wrinkling her brow as she always did when worried. "I expect that fathead of an ape dived in there for safety."

She peered in, but could see nothing. But far off she thought she could detect a pathetic whimper.

"Did I say I'd keep a zoo?" she asked herself in grim humour as she bunched her skirts to the front and tied a bit of string round herself to keep as clean as possible. "Here goes to bring you out, Marcus, my boy. And when I catch you I've a good mind to give you a couple of slaps for yourself!"

It took no little courage to crawl into that narrow space. There is something very terrible about pulling yourself along a narrow way, the roof just above your head, and the uncomfortable knowledge drumming in your brain that you can't turn round; you must either go on or go back, and neither way easy!

As soon as she was well into the drain, Merryl found that her ears were full of strange noises, for every tiny sound was magnified in that hollow space, so that dull boomings and shufflings filled the air. In places the stones of the drain had been forced apart by descending roots, which blocked the already narrow space with iron-hard bands, by which Merryl could only just squeeze.

"Don't panic!" she told herself sternly as the horrible idea of getting stuck came to haunt her. "I can do what a miserable ape can do. It can't be much further."

She felt she must have crawled for yards. Evidently the drain continued underground for some distance on the far side of the wall. She had an uneasy impression that it was getting narrower. It seemed to pin her elbows and knees, and all at once breathing was more difficult. Suppose a sudden thunderstorm filled the drain? Horrors! Could she get back?

"This is about the nastiest thing I've ever had to do," she thought, and then relief flooded through her. "Oh, goody, goody! Daylight!"

A blue blur ahead cheered her and suddenly the air was warmer. Through a greenish fringe of bracken she pushed her way and stood up.

"My—oh, boy!" was all that she could say for a minute. She had come some way from the wall and now stood in a secret garden. It must have been years since any gardener had worked here; bushes, plants and trees had long since burst out of all control and rioted altogether.

What had once been lawn was a waist-high tangle coarse as jungle undergrowth and starred by ox-eye daisies and the red plumes of sorrel. The herbaceous borders were a wealth of mixed bloom, hot and glorious, heavily scented and yet all bound together by festoons of bindweed whose huge white bells defied law and order.

Some fruit trees of the ornamental kind were shedding their late blossoms; the warm wind burdened by showers of petals swept over the grass and rained them at Merryl's feet. Just in front of her was an old stone sundial—and on the top, holding on to the gnomon, was Marcus.

He frustrated any ideas of punishment by giving a guttural little cry of joy and hurling himself at her to wind his arms about her neck as she stooped to kiss his bullet-head.

"Well, I'm so glad to see you, so I won't thump you this time," the girl said. "Oh, what a place for the zoo! Only a few hundred yards from home, in this deserted walled garden—oh, *what* a place!"

She paused to read the mottoes carved deeply in the stone surround of the sundial.

Free to us all are the wild flowers and the birdsong, the rising stars and moonset. But Time is precious, so use it wisely.

On the other side was the cryptic message:

The man who tries to cure some of the world's troubles has no time for his own.

"Oh, I wonder who used to live here," Merryl sighed. "It would have been fun knowing them. Anyway, that is the zoo accommodation nicely settled. No one could mind our using such a derelict place, only we shall have to find a better way in!"

"What on earth are you doing here?" a voice asked, and Merryl jumped. It was uncanny to hear things when she had thought she was alone. A girl, a little older and taller than herself, was wading through the tall grass. At her side a wiry terrier sprang along; he kept trying to leap up and snap playfully at her cardigan. She was swinging a tennis-racquet, with which she whacked at the daisy-heads in a petulant way as if she grudged them their place in the sun.

"And what's that black horror?" the girl went on, kicking at the dog to keep it behind her.

"That's Marcus, my pet ape, and I only came in to catch him. He ran off," Merryl explained.

"How did you get in?" A gleam of curiosity lighted the sullen discontent of the strange girl's face. "I thought *I* knew the only way in here!"

"D'you mean through the drain under the wall?" Merryl asked in great surprise. "Is this *really* a secret garden?"

"There never was any way into it except through the house, which is all standing empty now and shut up. If you came in by a drain, d'you mind going out again? I came here to practise and give Rupert his run, and I've some right here 'cause my uncle's the agent."

"Isn't that a bit mean?" Merryl remonstrated. "What harm are we doing, anyway?"

But before anyone could say another word, the terrier took charge of the situation. He had come bustling and shooting himself through the grass to

see who it was standing there and suddenly he saw
Marcus. He paused, stiffening all over, one paw
raised and still quivering with arrested eagerness,
his nose ridging cruelly as he growled thunderously.
Marcus viewed these preparations with mild astonishment and placed one hand over his face as if
he were convulsed with laughter. Between his black
fingers his eyes shone merrily.

"Guff, guff," he grunted amiably, which was
too much for the terrier.

He flung himself forward with a string of shattering barks, his ears flattened to his skull, his eyes
popping out with eagerness. Marcus removed his
hand from his face, knuckled the ground and began
to dance very softly up and down, his hind toes
curling inwards in his excitement. Guttural grunts
burst from him.

"Call off your dog!" Merryl shrieked, trying to
get in front of Marcus in time.

"*Rupert!*" screamed the new girl. "Come here
at once!"

But Rupert was deaf to entreaties, and he flung
himself at the ape, actually butting him over on the
grass. The terrier's teeth tried to snap at the ape's
tough hairy body, but somehow he could not get
in. Marcus had apparently gone mad! His mild-
ness vanished before this mean attack.

His arms whirled round his head like the sails
of a windmill and before the indignant terrier

realised which way the fortunes of battle were tending the ape had grabbed him up, and, holding him to his hairy chest as a mother clasps her straying child, galloped off, bounding through and over the high grass. Rupert's barks slid up the scale of sound from deep threats to the high notes of pure terror.

"Stop him, stop!" the strange girl wailed. "He'll kill my dog! Oh, only stop him and—and you can come here—I'll show you my own way in. Oh, oh, oh!"

"Don't be so soft!" Merryl cried, for in danger her wits always seemed to cool, and it was only afterwards that she would tremble and flush from nervous reaction. "Gimme that racquet! I may have to hit him over the head with something!"

She tore after Marcus and Rupert, and Milly Anderson brought up the rear, wringing her hands.

"*Marcus!*" Merryl called sharply, so sharply that the ape heard her and glanced over his shoulder, a sudden uneasy gleam in his dark eyes. She flourished the racquet menacingly. "Come here at once, you quarrelsome thing, and let that poor dog go!"

Now, the ape had a good memory. It was one of the most surprising things about him. He viewed that racquet in sudden trepidation. In shape it was extremely like that instrument of torture which earlier that day had been applied to him. His jaw dropped and his grasp relaxed. Rupert felt the pressure on his ribs ease off, and he slipped to the ground with furtive speed, then like a flash of light streaked back to his mistress, and only then, from the safety of her protection, barked a renewed challenge—but not so aggressively as before.

Merryl could not help smiling as a subdued little ape crept up to her, caught at her frock in his black fingers and looked up beseechingly.

"Okay; don't do it again," she soothed.

Milly was gazing pop-eyed and almost speechless. "Oh, I *say*!" she whispered. "D'you mean to say he's *tame*?" Envy lighted up her small green eyes.

"Well, tame enough," Merryl laughed, glad that all had ended so well, for she hated being unfriendly with anyone.

"May I pat him?" Milly did so gingerly, and Marcus grunted and Rupert cringed away and growled his jealousy. But Merryl was jubilant. The zoo had got its place all right!

"I'll take you up on what you said about coming here. My name's Merryl Penny."

Milly nodded and gave her own name. "I'll show you my own way in," she said, and picked up Rupert. "It is a jolly good thing he isn't hurt, for Uncle wants to show him for the Flaxstead Cup next week, in the best-pet-in-show class. He's sure he'll win. Rupert's a far finer dog than that silly old Roy of Connisdale from Carter's Farm, who got it last year."

"I'm showing Marcus," Merryl said, and could have screamed with laughter at the stunned expression on the other's face.

Milly, however, stuck loyally to her promise and led the way into a thick shrubbery where hazels and willows grew so closely together that it was like pushing through a jungle. But behind ran another section of the wall giving on to another road, and here the bricks were more weathered and had given way, undermined by oozy runlets of water. A portion of the wall had collapsed inwards to make a low mound, over which they scrambled.

Next day Merryl phoned the gang and told them of her find.

"Oh, boy!" Teddy jubilated into the phone. "I say, this is *it*!"

"Stop shouting and listen. About the Show! I'm determined to enter Marcus. Can you all come over the day before and we'll groom him for stardom."

"Of course we can. What d'you mean—groom him for stardom?" Teddy asked suspiciously.

"Oh, his fur's full of dried mud; he never looks where he's going. I've combed handfuls of goose-grass burrs from behind his ears!" And Merryl rang off.

When the day came, Merryl began heating water directly after breakfast, for she was determined that Marcus should have a bath. She had bought a hair-shampoo packet, and with this whisked up a tubful of lovely suds. Marcus, suddenly apprehensive, pottered about, grumbling audibly, hooding his brows over his liquid eyes, and picking uneasily at his twitching lips.

The gang burst into Bramble Cottage bearing gifts: a beautiful waistbelt of hand-plaited leather, which Giles the cowman had made, and a light dog-chain.

"He's going to look super." Merryl thanked them. "Now, Marcus. Where is he?—the bath's ready."

They caught the terrified ape just as he was about to bolt out of the toolshed, and by brute force he was plunged into the tub. Afterwards, Merryl found time to regret that they had not protected themselves. When you are trying to hold down a [scared ape in a nice warm bath of soap and water, and the animal is resisting with spirit, waves are set up which slop everywhere with the direst results.

They rubbed him, and he screamed and bit the bath-flannel into holes; he clung to the sides of the tub with fingers so strong that they could not be unlocked when they wanted him to turn round. They rinsed him with a watering-can and when he was finished each one of them was soaked to the skin, their shoes squelching, the toolshed floor a mass of yellow mud, and Marcus almost out of his mind.

But a brisk towelling in front of the electric heater in the living-room, and the ape felt better, and certainly he looked it. In his new belt and chain he appeared what he really was: a very fine specimen, probably worth quite a lot of money.

When they had changed and Aunt Penny had loaned them dressing-gowns and coats while she dried their things, they went at Marcus again. They rubbed hand-cream into his leathery palms to make them soft and smooth. Marcus rather liked it, and he smelled like a florist's after it.

They managed to get him to the Show grounds the next day without his soiling himself in any way, which was an extraordinary thing. Milly and her uncle were there, and she waved condescendingly to them and they could see her pointing them out to the tall man at her side. He looked across at them with undisguised interest.

But Merryl's heart had sunk as far as Marcus's prospects were concerned. The very cream of the world of pets was being chained up in the places set aside for dogs, or bolted into the special huts for the cats and other creatures. Long and short-haired queens of the feline world, huge dogs, and tiny toy varieties, each one was perfection in its own way.

"Anyway, Marcus is the only ape," Teddy whispered, but his tone admitted that he did not expect any red-and-gold rosettes on Marcus's hutch.

"What about another animal for the zoo?" Dodie said softly. "I do wish we could afford to buy one of those Alsatians. They are beauties!"

Two of them were being led past at that minute, and Marcus pranced up and down and made rude noises.

"He hates dogs after that fuss the other day," Merryl explained, and she wished that people would not push and jostle so. Everywhere owners were giving last touches to their pets. At one hutch, some ten feet away, a big farmy-looking woman was giving a peke one last gentle brushing and using a real hairbrush for it, at sight of which the ape began to squeal thinly through his nose to show that he had not forgotten his humiliation.

"For goodness' sake look out or there's going to be trouble," Ken breathed. "There, they are beginning the judging. Let's take Marcus along now and get it over!"

"You can't," Merryl pointed out, "not till his class comes up."

So they shut him into a disused hutch and joined the people at the judging ring. Terriers were being shown. Each beast, groomed to perfection and walking almost stiffly in the pride of champion pedigrees, slowly circled the ring, led round by their anxious owners.

On a stand at the back stood the magnificent Flaxstead Cup, and Merryl, looking at it, wondered uneasily if it stood perfectly square, or was one of its ball feet slightly flattened against the body of the cup itself?

"Don't be a fathead," she scolded herself.

The judge now singled out five of the best terriers which had to parade again, but Rupert was not among them, for he was in another age-group.

"I say," Ken chuckled wickedly, "what will the judge say to an ape? I can hardly wait."

Class after class was judged, and the air in the big tent grew sultry, the dogs fretful, and their owners hot and sticky. No one knew quite what happened, but just as the Alsatians were being called there was an uproar at the doorway leading into the other tent where the exhibition animals were being housed.

A huge Alsatian burst out and charged down into the crowd. People screamed and held back to let it go bounding past. It could have been caught by anyone possessing a bit of ready courage. A second dog, an Airedale, and evidently the aggressor, came after it chopping and foaming, a broken lead whipping from its collar.

A smother of growls and snarling and worrying sounds rose as the two went into a clinch at the end of the tent. Merryl and the gang tried to reach the spot, for all knew that if the dogs were not parted at once one of them was going to be hurt. Merryl was not scared of dogs, and the farm children were used to handling Nimmo, the big bull, and far more dangerous animals than a couple of scrapping dogs.

But before they could get anywhere near, something black flashed past. A woman let out an hysterical whimper of laughter and a man shouted to the crowd to catch the escaping monkey. But Marcus was not to be caught. How he had got his hutch open no one could say. The fact remained that he was evidently determined to mix it with the dogs. He was waving something in one hand, and Merryl could just make out what it was—a hairbrush—probably the very one the woman with the peke had been using.

The ape took a flying leap and landed on the neck of the Alsatian. Both dogs were blind and deaf to their surroundings as they thrashed round in a whirl of dust of their own making. But Marcus had no intention of allowing this to go on. He was bored and scared and he *hated* dogs. This whole place reeked of dogs, and it raised in him a wild revolt.

So he clung to the neck of the maddened dog and he hammered on its skull with the wooden-backed hairbrush. *Thwack, thwack*—the blows could be heard all over the tent. No doubt Marcus was wiping from the slate of his memory the indignity offered to his own person by Miss Penny when she spanked him.

"*Marcus!*" Merryl screamed in desperation, afraid that her pet would be annihilated.

But almost anything can be done to animals when they are really fighting without their noticing a thing. *Bang, thwack*—the brush came down again and again, and at last the dog began to realise dimly that something outside of itself was getting very uncomfortable. It backed off for a moment, shaking its dizzy head, for its wits were buzzing like a nest of wasps. Marcus crowed with joy and flung his arms round the dog's neck, hugging in a transport of delight and finishing off the fight effectually, for the dog, feeling itself being throttled, turned rolling and gnashing, trying to unseat this demon on its neck.

The other dog, too, thankful for a chance of escaping the consequences of its own attack, backed cringing into the crowd, its tail between its legs. Its owner hastily dragged it out of harm's way. So just as the stewards of the Show rushed up with pails of water, the fight was done.

The Alsatian, with Marcus 'up', looked round frenziedly, and seeing the open countryside through a flap of the tent made a dash for it, thinking to knock off or brush off the rider on its neck.

"Catch them," roared a man's voice, and Merryl recognised the owner of the Airedale. She had noticed him earlier, when the dogs were parading.

She and the gang rushed from the tent, followed

by the man and one or two others. The terrified
dog was streaking out of sight, but the four raced
after it, frightened that once the creature slowed
down and stopped panicking it would turn and
massacre the ape. Over the brow of a low hill
they tore, for the Show was being held in some
fields outside Flaxstead. Teddy was ahead, running
like a champion. And then they came on Marcus.

He was sitting on the ground looking a trifle
dazed and gazing gloomily at the splintered handle
of the hairbrush, which was all that was left to
him. He kept shaking his head as if bewildered by
the pace at which he had been going. The Airedale's
owner caught up with them.

"Where's the other dog?" he demanded, and
they could not make out from his tone exactly what
he was feeling. He sounded furious, but Merryl
did not think it was all against them, as, after all, it
was their pet which had saved the situation.

"You're the Carter boys, aren't you?" he shouted
at Teddy and Ken. "I'll see you after the Show."
And he was off after the dog his Airedale had tried
to kill.

Merryl could have wept when they examined the
exhausted ape. All his smartness had vanished
utterly. All their love and care had gone for nothing.
Several scratches were bleeding freely, and the
blood had mixed with the dust to make a kind of
rich paste, with which Marcus's hair seem fairly

well plastered. The ribbon which Dodie had insisted on tying round his neck, for she said that the red satiny gleam of it showed up so well, now hung in damp, limp ends. He was tired out and dejected, as he always was after stenuous action.

As soon as they had done examining him, he held up weary little arms and gave a dismal little grunt. Merryl it was who carried him back, and he clung whining to her while the gang trailed along behind, their spirits in their boots.

They met Milly taking Rupert back to be tied up in the other tent. The dog was grinning with canine pride, ears a-cock, beady black eyes flashing with health and fitness. Milly looked her concern at the sight of the ape's messy coat, but she could not help tossing her head with satisfaction over her own possible triumph.

"This is Milly," Merryl said to the others, who did not seem to be much impressed. "Was the judge pleased with Rupert?"

Milly gave a little hooting kind of laugh. "He couldn't very well help himself," she said with conscious superiority. "My Rupert can trace his pedigree back for *miles*! I expect we shall get the cup. After all, it is the best that should win, don't you agree?"

"Of course," Teddy said suddenly, his face flushing dangerously. "That's why I shall be amazed if that scruff-pot of yours wins!"

There was a deep silence. Then: "*Oh!*" cried Milly, outraged, and she flounced away, taking Rupert with her.

After that the gang felt a little better, but nothing could hide their coming defeat from them. Dodie even suggested shamefacedly sneaking out and going home now, as there was no use in waiting, but the others were made of tougher stuff. At last the notice for the final class went up, when anyone could be judged for the best pet in the Show.

"Come on, Marcus," Merryl said ruefully, for anything less like a champion you could not imagine. Marcus was all tuckered out. After all, he was only very young. He snuggled and sighed and refused to be roused. Merryl entered the ring and put the ape down gently to parade with the others. There was a smothered ejaculation from the watchers, and someone laughed, but not unkindly.

Holding to her hand and looking round him vacant-eyed and sleepy, Marcus shuffled along, one hand to his mouth fingering his lips just like a shy child. After they had circled the floor, the judge signalled to ten of them to retire. Merryl was not sure whether or no Marcus had been included, so she was turning away when the man signed to her to wait with the other five for a second scrutiny. Milly's eyebrows went up and a sneer curved her mouth and she managed to convey by her glance that her opinion of the judge had sustained a severe blow. The men took a long time making up their minds, but at last they cleared the ring and compared notes, while Milly patted Rupert and led him away joyfully.

"What happens now?" Merryl asked. "How do we know?"

"Well, here they usually go round and fix the ribbons on the winners while lunch is served in the other tent. They don't let anyone in," Teddy explained. "But you needn't worry. Milly's little brute was the best in that fifteen!"

They ate their lunch in silence and found very little flavour in the chicken and salad. Just as they were leaving the tent a man stopped them.

"Look here, didn't I say I wanted to see you?"

Teddy faced him defiantly and the others tried to back him up by appearing stolidly hostile. A flash of surprise dawned in the man's eyes.

"I say, you do all look sulky!" he went on. "And I thought you'd be pleased." He took out a notebook and extracted four one-pound notes. "If your blooming monkey hadn't broken up that fight when he did I should have had serious trouble over my Rex, for this isn't his first scrap. I feel I owe you four quite a lot. So will you get yourselves something with that or go to the pictures till it's used up? Eh? Just a mark of gratitude!"

"What?" Teddy gasped. "Oh, I say, thanks, sir! May we do what we like with it?"

"Of course! I said so; there's no stick attached. Why?"

"Zoo funds!" they all yelled, and then they had to explain. The man looked astounded.

"The modern kids beat all!" he exclaimed and walked away.

"Oh, the zoo can begin any time," Merryl cried, her eyes dancing. With her golden curls all ruffled and blowing about her face as she stood there she looked a picture, but she did not know and would not have cared if she had known. "We've a place for it and four quid to start it. And that dear, good, clever Marcus of ours has done it all himself. He's our mascot! Oh, whoopee!"

"What a bit of luck out of the blue like that," Dodie gasped, and Ken suggested that they all celebrate with an ice apiece.

"But not bought out of the zoo funds," cried the treasurer in quick alarm. They got an ice for Marcus, and carried it joyfully into the other tent, where the prize marking was over and people were streaming back to their charges.

"Come and see," Milly crowed, and led them to the bench where Rupert was chained. Even on the dog's face was an expression of insufferable satisfaction, as if he knew his worth. Pinned on his card was a large red-and-gold rosette and the words: FLAXSTEAD CUP.

"Well done," Merryl remarked cheerfully.

"Don't let Marcus get hold of the cup, will you? He nearly bust it once before." She could not feel jealousy or petty disappointment, for she was so happy that the zoo could be launched.

"What *do* you mean?" Milly cried, her face darkening. "If I thought that that grubby ape of yours had even so much as seen the cup I'd not have it."

"Then you would be more of a fathead than I thought," Teddy cried frankly, and they left her fuming and wondering what they meant.

They bore his ice to Marcus in triumph and jubilation. As they neared his hutch they found a small knot of people looking at him, for, outside a zoo, you don't see many of these funny little odd-faced creatures.

Marcus had waked up feeling better, and he was acknowledging their admiration with a charming grace. He waved his arms, jabbered his mobile lips at them and scratched ecstatically.

"Hull*o*!" Teddy gasped. "What on earth is that on the floor of his hutch?"

"He must have pulled it off and dragged it inside," a woman explained. "But I didn't like to recover it. I didn't know if he was dangerous!"

Stupefied, Merryl reached in and rescued the blue and gold of a second-prize rosette.

"Marcus, you *darling*!" Dodie cried, and the onlookers smiled good-humouredly. Now indeed the day was very bright! And when, half an hour later, they were on their way home it was difficult to keep from yelling their triumph to the summer woods. The ape was as pleased as anyone, and so he should be!

He might well have reasoned that arms were long and fingers nimble because Nature intended them to be used. It had been so easy when the judges stood a moment outside his hutch admiring him in passing on their way to sneak out his black leathery hand and nip up one of those delightful coloured trifles off the tray. With deep cunning he hid what he had done until they had passed on and then he sat admiring his lovely booty, stroking it with care, staring out at the other animals and hooding his brows over his liquid eyes.

CHAPTER 3

THE AMAZING TREK

MERRYL collected the letters off the mat and carried them into the front room, where Miss Penny was helping Marcus with his breakfast. The ape had been much better behaved for the last week, and, as he sat at the table on her tallest chair, supplemented by the dictionary and an atlas, he appeared quite a pattern of manners. He dug and scooped at his porridge, grunting to encourage himself when the, to him, extremely inadequate tool slipped and splashed warm milk into his earnest face.

"Isn't he sweet?" Merryl sighed.

Her aunt glanced at the handwriting on the letters. "Why there's one from your great-uncle Bob. He hasn't written to me three times in the last five years. I sent him a line last week telling him all about your zoo. Let's see what he says. He was always passionately fond of animals."

She inserted the bread-knife into the top of the envelope and sliced the paper apart. Marcus stopped eating to watch keenly, dribbling milk unreproved. Miss Penny's eyes darted through the words of the letter, and a doubtful smile, in which lurked a faint apprehension, touched her lips.

"Oh, Merryl, I hardly know what to answer," she said as two pasteboard slips fell from the pages.

Merryl was all agog. "Railway tickets?" she asked in surprise. She picked one up. "Singles to Comthorpe, in Yorkshire?"

"Yes, dear. Comthorpe is where Uncle Bob lives, but, dear me, I feel all upset!"

"Oh, do tell me," Merryl cried, hardly able to eat her cereal.

Miss Penny read: "Dear Agatha, I must say I was pleased to get your letter and I am absolutely delighted in the enterprise shown by my great-niece, the more so as it makes something easy for me which otherwise was rather an obstacle. An old friend of mine has invited me to go out to New Zealand for an extensive holiday and I have accepted. Indeed, when you read this I shall be on my way to London. I enclose an address there where I shall be for the next few days, so you can wire me if Merryl accepts my proposition. Otherwise, as I cannot take him with me, I must send word to have Diccon put to sleep, as I will not have him go to anyone I do not know and who might be unkind to him. What I thought was that if Merryl and, say, one friend for company could come up to Comthorpe at once they can have Diccon for the zoo. My good housekeeper, Mrs. Travers, will be at

this address for the next week, after which if no one
has called for him she will have Diccon painlessly
destroyed. I have arranged the details for her. My
love, Robert Penny."

"Oh!" Merryl cried, clasping her hands together
and feeling that she wanted to dance and shout with
excitement. "Oh, how priceless! But he never said
what Diccon is. From the name I should say a
canary!"

"That's exactly like Bob. Absent-minded but
good-hearted to a fault!"

Merryl was examining the tickets again. Her
face was flushed with mixed feelings, her eyes shone.
"I can't understand *single* tickets!"

Her aunt regarded her in troubled doubt. "My
dear, Diccon may be a mangy old dog or a decrepit
cat past mice and only wanting to feed and sleep."

"That makes it all rather more fun. The only
thing that is worrying me is if you will find Marcus
too much for you while I am away."

"I don't suppose I shall," her aunt remarked
almost dryly, then smiled at Merryl's dismay. "No,
dear, I'm only troubling about you. But if you really
want to save poor Diccon's life, whom will you take?"

"Dodie!"

"Then I can't allow you to go," Miss Penny said
firmly. "If you will take Teddy I'll consent. He has
a very good head for his age, and it's a long journey.
You will? Then you'd better telegraph Bob!"

Merryl got her bike out and raced to Flaxstead, and sent the words that were to save poor Diccon speeding to London. Then she went to Carter's Farm to call a hurried meeting.

"Who's going with you?" they all cried, eager hope in each pair of eyes.

"Teddy," Merryl said, and Teddy immediately began throwing handsprings. The others tried pluckily to hide their disappointment and accept the president's decision.

"Anyway, we shall be waiting all in a thrill for you to get back," Dodie cried. "I'm going to get all that rank growth in the secret garden scythed away. I can scythe better than Giles—Dad said so —and Ken and Milly can begin to put up some shelters. Dad says we can have the old planking from the ruined barn and some tarpaulin covers off the hay, and he'll lend us the two horses, Wednesday, to get the stuff to the place!"

"That's absolutely super," Merryl cried in delight. "We shall be able to have the opening soon, at this rate."

Milly hove in sight here and joined them without a word. She was given to creeping quietly about wherever she wanted, and in this case it was a proof of her envious desire to join in with the absorbing new game.

"Hello, Mill!" Teddy shouted, getting up off the grass, on to which he had collapsed in exhaustion.

"I asked my father," Milly began primly, for she was not quite sure of her reception, "and he said he saw no harm in our playing in the secret garden even if he is the agent for the place, and the owner is abroad and hates the place, anyway."

"Play?" Merryl asked dubiously. "You were going to ask if we could keep animals there!"

"Sometime," Milly answered airily. "Now, can I be a member?"

"It's hard work," Ken said wickedly, looking at Milly's plump little hands, all white and smooth. There was a rumour going round the irrepressible gang that Milly had a maid to brush her teeth for her.

Tears of disappointment welled in Milly's eyes and her mouth turned down mutinously. "I think you are a set of pigs if you don't let me help."

"Okay," Teddy answered easily. "What say, President?"

"I say, let Milly in," Merryl cried warmly, and the others nodded good-naturedly. Only Ken, with an evil leer, returned to the barn to look out his carpentry tools.

Teddy and Merryl set out for the station early the next morning. They biked along the country lanes, where the world of men was only just waking, though the birds had been holding a clamorous concert since four. Heavy dew twinkled on the grass, as if someone had broken a necklace of gems and scattered them. The shadows lay all the wrong way round; the air was warm and sweet with summer scents.

They put their bikes into the luggage-room at the station. When the train had clanked round the bend and chuff-chuffed to a stop, the engine perspiring profusely, they climbed in.

"This is larks!" Merryl said. "I've never been north before. What time do we get there?"

"Four-thirty," Teddy replied. "Oh, I wonder what Diccon is. I have an awful fear that the canary theory is going to hold true. Shan't we look nitwits walking in at home with a blooming bird in a tin cage?"

All through the long morning the train snored and bored its way north through some of the loveliest country in England. At noon they walked along and lunched in the restaurant car, which in itself was a bit of a lark. But though neither of them would confess it both felt forlorn and lost when at last they walked out of the station at Comthorpe into the afternoon bustle of a busy market-town.

Now Merryl was glad that Teddy was with her, for his sturdy presence gave her a lot of comfort. How purposeful the people looked, all hurrying along and never stopping to give a glance or a friendly greeting! Teddy was feeling desolate, too, for his mouth set in a certain grim way it had. Silently he got out the slip of paper with the address written on it.

"I wonder what Marcus is doing," Merryl said

wistfully, and then an awful possibility made her go quite cold. Suppose Diccon were another ape? Oh, no, it couldn't be so awful! Not that two apes were too much for the zoo, but variety is everything and she felt quite reasonably that one ape was as much as they could cope with. But they had given their word that Diccon should have a good home and not be put to sleep in untimely haste. A telegram thanking them warmly had come from London yesterday, and so they were committed.

"Forty-two Grange Road. We'll have a taxi," Teddy said firmly. "It's always quickest in a new town."

"What a cold, hard, bright sort of place," Merryl said, flattening her nose against the window as they bowled along. "D'you know, I don't think I should care to live here, somehow!"

The taxi came to a stop outside number forty-two. Grange Road was on the outskirts of the town, where the houses stood in spacious gardens and among prosperous farms.

"It's a cow, perhaps," Teddy choked suddenly as they tumbled out.

"Want me to wait?" the man asked as Teddy paid him.

"Er, no—I don't think so, thanks."

An old woman with a lined face like a white walnut answered the knocker. "Ah, you'll be the Penny children!"

"No, *I'm* Merryl Penny and this is a friend!"

"Come in, come in! Master told me to look after you. I've yer teas ready!"

Tea! Their spirits rose, and only then did they realise that much of their low spirits had been ravenous hunger. Mrs. Travers led them into a snug back room, where a generous urn of tea was flanked by plates of hot buttered muffins, a dish of ham and eggs sizzling quietly over a hot-plate, and a bowl of early strawberries with sugar and cream. She tactfully left them to enjoy it all alone.

"My stars," Teddy cried vulgarly, "what a tasteful blow-out! After this, I don't care if Diccon's a rhinoceros!"

Feeling stuffed and sleepy they carried the cups and plates into the kitchen and won Mrs. Travers's heart by helping with the washing-up as a matter of course.

"Now I'll show you your bedrooms, dearies," she said, "and then you'll likely want to see yer new pet. What time do you want to start back?"

"That depends," Teddy said cautiously, for he did not know if they might have to get a crate for Diccon.

She led the way out into what was evidently the yard of a big farm and across the flags to a big barn. She unlocked the door, which swung open to let out the sickly sweet smell of damp hay and straw, and another smell which neither Teddy nor Merryl could place: a leathery, mousy, doggy smell.

In the dimness of the half light a huge beast shuffled its feet, shackled with a chain to a fixed pin. It rolled inquisitive little eyes at them. There was a dry swishy sound as it whisked an absurd tail.

"Diccon is a beauty," Mrs. Travers said fondly. "I shall be right sorry to see him go. That intelligent he is! Would obey the master as if they two spoke the same language!"

"An *elephant*!" Merryl almost screamed. Her breath strangled in her throat. Delight and terror were mixed in her tones.

"*What?*" Teddy howled, bounding into the barn as if he could not believe his eyes.

"Yes, didn't you know?" Mrs. Travers asked in amazement. "I understood from the master that you were brought up in some zoo or other and knew all about animals."

Sheer pride prevented them from giving her the facts and dispelling this exciting fancy.

"Of course we understand animals," Teddy said stoutly. "Diccon is a fine beast and we'll get him off tomorrow."

A great light dawned on Merryl. "Teddy, the single tickets," she whispered. "Do you realise that Diccon will have to go by road?"

"Eh, what's that?" Teddy cried, aghast at this revelation. The miles that lay between them and home seemed to have lengthened and lengthened so that it seemed impossible that they could be back at Bramble Cottage this time next week. Mrs. Travers had gone indoors, and for a long time the two sat on upturned buckets in the barn staring in consternation at Diccon, who chewed slowly and thoughtfully and watched them with keen speculation in his little eyes.

Merryl's dreams that night were anything but peaceful, for she found herself mixed up in the most awful adventures, in which a great elephant loomed menacingly, so that she woke, shaking at the memory and overcome at the thought of the responsibilities they had so lightly undertaken.

After breakfast, which was a rich meal, for Mrs. Travers evidently believed in working on a full stomach, they asked her about Diccon's food. She seemed surprised, as if she expected them to know all about that, but cheerfully gave them directions as to what the elephant was accustomed to eating. Merryl was secretly appalled at the amount. She knew that Teddy had brought some of the zoo funds with him for Diccon and wondered uneasily how they were going to manage if they ran through it. A new respect, hitherto never felt nor thought of, came to her for the folk who ran the great institution for animals in Regent's Park.

Mrs. Travers came with them to the barn to say goodbye to her charge.

"He's had his breakfast," she explained, and showed them how to knock the pin out of his

c

shackles so that the chain could be slipped off. Merryl said she'd carry the gear, but Teddy said they'd take turns.

"He's as good as gold; leastways he always was with master," the woman assured them, as if she thought there was doubt in their faces. Diccon curled up his trunk, gave a thin little 'blerrup' in his nose as if he were excited, and began backing ponderously towards the door, but watching over his own shoulder, so to speak, and moving with such nicety and exactness that he never bumped once.

"So long." The woman waved to them when they were at last in the road.

"How—er—do we lead him?" Teddy asked desperately, his pride giving way at last under the pressure of unusual circumstances.

"Just walk beside him or ride on his neck, as you please," Mrs. Travers called brightly and closed the door.

"Jumping pink eels!" Teddy breathed heavily. "This, Merry, is the first time I've ever been elephant boy and personally I'm feeling sticky with fright. What happens tonight if no one will take us in? What happens if Diccon acts ugly or——?"

"I don't think that need worry us," Merryl said, for as she walked along she had been looking up at Diccon and caught the expression in his little pig-like eyes, which were fixed on her. Almost she fancied that there was a good-humoured twinkle in their depths. "I believe he's as good as gold, truly!"

She patted the long trunk hanging down quietly so near her. At once the elephant stopped dead in his tracks.

"Now you've done it," Teddy cried crossly. "That must be his signal for a halt. Here, gerrup you, get a move on! Go on!"

But slaps and prods were of no avail. Diccon stood there patiently as if waiting for something. Merryl patted the trunk again, hoping to undo the mischief of the mistaken signal. Instantly it began to curl. Some memory of a jungle film seen once long ago in London made her give a little squeak of excitement. Being one who would always experiment, even when it entailed flirting with danger or what looked like danger, she stepped up into the loop the elephant was making for that purpose. Next instant and she was soaring aloft, held safely but rather tightly in the grip of Diccon's trunk. She landed on his neck quite breathless with the thrill, and she laughed as she looked down at Teddy standing gazing pop-eyed in the road.

"Oh, I *say*!" the boy cried. "Here, I'm coming up too. Saving of shoe-leather."

But to his consternation and disgust, no sooner was Merryl seated than Diccon began plodding forward again, and Teddy had to run to catch up.

"Here, you, stop!" he cried in great indignation,

and he patted the elephant's trunk. But either he did not pat gently enough or else Diccon was in teasing mood, but the animal refused to help him. So Teddy was forced to slog along in the dust whileMerryl rode. She could not help seeing the funny side of it.

"Poor old Ted—what a shame!" she cried.

"It's all very well sitting up there making pretty noises," he said. "My feet are getting positively sore. I expect they'll shrivel up and drop off and I shall just crawl unnoticed into a ditch and expire while you two go back to Bramble Cottage laughing your silly heads off. I'm certain Diccon's laughing now. There's a perfectly inane expression in his beady little eye!"

It seemed a very long morning, and, as they began meeting more traffic, curious glances were shot at them. People in cars turned to look back at them, pointing and talking. Luckily the elephant appeared quite used to traffic. He kept on the correct side of the road and moved on steadily enough.

But Merryl began to think from one or two little incidents that Diccon was rather self-willed and was only going with them now because for some obscure reason of his own it suited him to. They could not know that he was homesick for his master and was perhaps thinking in his limited way that he might find him out in the big world.

Merryl shivered at the thought of what might happen if Diccon for any reason should decide to take any road which they did not want. Her uneasy reflections were broken into by Teddy.

"There's a big farmhouse sort of place ahead. What say if we call a halt for lunch?"

"Famous! How do we stop Diccon?"

"Dunno," the boy said moodily, but there was a stubborn threat in his voice as he shouted at the elephant: "*Right wheel!*" meanwhile pushing against his trunk with hard hands.

Diccon paused, looked about him as if undecided and then spied some extremely nice hay being carted to a barn at the back of the house. His mind made up, he plodded into the yard. They had both forgotten to ask Mrs. Travers when his next meal was due, but it was too late now. He came to a stop and trumpeted loudly to attract attention. Merryl, who had not expected this, nearly fell off.

A fat old farmer bustled out and held up his hands in amazement.

"It's all right, sir," Teddy explained hurriedly. "Can you give us some lunch and sell us some hay and vegetables for Diccon?"

The old man staved off a fit by an almost visible effort and retired into the house to roar for 'mother', who, when she came, was almost as upset. Merryl slid down off the elephant's back and went forward with Teddy.

Once certain that the beast was harmless, the old couple showed their delight by bringing all the field-hands from the shed where they were lunching in order that they might not miss the fun. Hay, swedes and cabbage were brought for Diccon. Indoors the two travellers were asked to join the old couple at their meal, and they found how delicious stewed mutton followed by apple-tart can be when you are hungry on a fine summer's morning. The farmer would not take anything in payment except for Diccon's lunch, and they thanked the children so warmly and begged them to come again so heartily that it was evident that the little incident had provided matter for story and gossip for many long days to come.

Merryl and Teddy stood watching the elephant dealing with the last bits of his meal, two cabbages and a swede. The former he carved for himself by deliberately lowering a massive forefoot on to them so that they crashed apart in juicy green-white fragments, which he ladled up with his sensitive trunk and stuffed into his mouth. The swede gave him more trouble. It rolled about under his foot and proved tougher than he had expected. But no swede that ever grew could long withstand that weight and soon it too went the way of the greens.

"Now it's my turn to ride," Teddy exclaimed with some heat when all the farm-folk had assembled to see the start. "Here, Diccon, give us a trunk."

Merryl stood back, for she was sorry for tired

Teddy and wanted him to have the fun of seeing the world from an elephant's neck. But once again Diccon showed that only if what they wanted fitted in with his desires would he oblige them. He would shift from his own ways for no one.

"You'd better watch out, lad; yon's a queer-tempered beast," the farmer cried.

So they must start out on foot once more, turning to wave a last goodbye to the kind folk at the farm. The miles slowly unwound before them, and as they walked south, watching the signposts and working from one big town to another, they tried to calculate how long it would take them to reach home. By evening they had covered some thirty miles, and even Diccon looked as if he thought enough was as good as a feast. But they had struck a very lonely district. Moorland rolled away on every hand to a purple horizon, behind which an orange-and-gold sunset was fading out of the sky.

"It's ten miles to the next town. There's nothing for it; we must camp out here."

"Okay," Merryl said cheerfully, for she had thought that something like this might happen and had made a few purchases in a village five miles back while Teddy had had his hands full trying to keep the local children from under the elephant's feet. He did not know that they were perfectly safe, that no elephant will tread on anything, so cleverly sensitive are their big feet. But he did not know, and it looked dangerous, and he was in a hot perspiration fearing some accident, so that he was inclined to grumble at Merryl wanting to shop. But now he freely forgave her. She produced a bottle of milk and some pork-pies, so they turned into a nearby field and tethered Diccon for the night. Then, after eating their supper under the stars, they each selected a cosy-looking haystack and sank into it to sleep.

It was the oddest thing that Merryl had ever done. In towns one never thought of sleeping out of doors. She kept waking with a start, wondering where on earth she was, only to be more bewildered than ever, for overhead the quiet stars winked coldly, and against the velvet of the summer night-sky loomed the lumpy outlines of Diccon, swaying at his pickets and dreaming of the lovely hay he could not reach.

When she woke in the morning with the sun shining golden into her eyes she sat up to see Teddy astride his pile of hay doing calculations in his notebook.

"What's up, Ted?"

"Well, at the rate we're moving it's going to take us all of a week to get back to Flaxstead, and if Diccon wants feeding on the scale of yesterday we're gonna be pretty low in spot cash."

"This is awful," she cried. "We shall just have to live as cheaply as possible."

"Even then we must eat," Teddy hinted darkly. "Well, we may as well get a move on."

Diccon looked his astonishment at being ordered to take the road with nothing inside him, and they could not explain that this was not meanness on their part but simply lack of anywhere to buy food.

"You shall have some breakfast later," Merryl soothed, but the elephant eyed her coldly, disgust in his eyes.

They had sent off a telegram yesterday to the home people, and now they wondered as they tramped along what they were all doing at Carter's Farm and Bramble Cottage. It was all so far away, for here even the hedgerow flowers were different from home. Only the birdsong was the same.

Diccon was slouching along in what was evidently as near a bad temper as his placid nature would allow. He grunted and rumbled to himself, and now and again he curled up his trunk to nibble up a lock of hay clinging to the bushes and stuff it into his mouth, as if demonstrating that he was breakfastless.

"Well, so are we," Merryl reasoned with him, but the pachyderm did not appear to see this. She patted his trunk, but whether he was really dense this morning or no he refused to take the hint.

At noon they came to a more populated district, and Teddy sighed his relief. Telegraph-poles showed where the railway ran; a largish village spread over the hill, and some farm-buildings were clustered in a hollow. At the first farm they turned into the yard, as they had done yesterday, and, leaving Diccon in the yard, went into a barn to find someone.

There was a wild clatter behind them as if someone had dropped many pails, a loud scream, and a thundering rush. They raced out to find a farm-woman leaning on the pump-handle for support, her round face the same colour as her apron. The elephant was nowhere to be seen.

"Oh, what's wrong? Diccon didn't hurt you, did he?" Merryl asked in an agony of terror.

When the woman had got her second wind, she shook her head. "No, that's all right," she whispered querulously. "But I were not expecting an empy in the yard and the sight of him fair give me the staggers. So I up and threw my pails at him and off he goes!"

"*What?*" Teddy yelled. "You frightened him, you old fathead?"

"He'd frightened me," she cried, blazing out in anger. "And if you two don't pack off this minute I'll phone for the perlice. What was you doing in that barn, anyway?"

But they had gone already, running down the road in great dismay, for there was no sign of their new pet.

"He can't be far; he's too big," wailed Merryl, reflecting as she ran that if they met anyone and asked him if he had seen an elephant it would get about that they were 'bats'.

"I say, look, he went through here," Teddy cried. In the muddy pathway into a field was a huge imprint. They ran over the stubble, flushing indignant larks and yellowhammers.

"There he is!" Merryl gasped as she caught a glimpse of the elephant's grey back.

He was down in the deep ditch between the field and the single-track railway line, stuffing himself with hay; where it had been cut recently, a long swathe of the thick grasses had fallen over the bank.

"Oh, Diccon, how could you?" Merryl said almost tearfully. He heard, and lifted his huge ears, and gave a little squeal as if in warning. Not for the first time did a sense of the tremendous responsibilities they had undertaken so carelessly rush over her to damp her spirits. "Teddy, he sounds quite peevish," she said nervously. "Suppose he won't obey us and come back on the road? You know he has a will of his own, and yet Mrs. Travers said he was so obedient!"

"Expect he is with anyone he knows. We'll let him eat and then we'll try when he's in a better temper."

So when the elephant had consumed all the hay in sight and was gazing round eagerly for more, Teddy ran up to him and slapped one sturdy, column-like leg.

"Gerrup, old man. Time to be off!"

Diccon looked round at the boy, who confessed afterwards that he was never in such a blue funk in all his days as he was under that reproachful scrutiny from those small intelligent eyes. He braced himself to stare back, to out-stare Diccon, for had not some adventure-writer in some boys' book said that you must never let animals win by glancing away from them in fear? Presently, Diccon grew weary and shuffled to get his bulk out of the ditch, but, alas, on the wrong side!

He quickly burst his way through the stranded wire and mounted swiftly on to the actual track, where, finding the going straight and interesting, he continued to plod along, head nodding, tail swishing its comic little length, as if he were suddenly determined to set off and get somewhere.

Merryl had thought things were as bad as they could be and now learned the sad lesson that they can sometimes be worse. She clutched at Teddy's arm. Her face was drawn and pale and she was shaking.

"Oh, what are we to do?"

"Get him off!" Teddy shouted. "Now run, Merry, as fast as you never did before."

They caught him up and tried to head him off. They danced upon the track in front of him, but he looked his surprise at them, brushed gently past them and went on purposefully as if in his dim way he realised that tracks meant a way for traffic and so were the right things to travel along.

"What if a train comes?" Merryl groaned.

"Driver'd see him. Couldn't miss!"

"Not if it were on a bend—he'd have no time. A heavy train can't pull up suddenly under so many hundred yards. There was something about it in the paper once."

"Look here, there's one way," Teddy said gravely. "Read it in a book, but you've got to have grit." He explained quickly, and Merryl nodded. "He can get past one, but if we link hands he'll have to stop. They won't deliberately knock you down. Only you *must* hold on however he seems to be towering over you, and I must say he can look ugly."

As he talked, they were running to get ahead again and meanwhile Diccon ambled on, his small eyes rolling at the scenery, his ears cocking and lowering like fans.

"*Now!*" Teddy cried when they were twenty yards ahead.

They linked hands and stretched out their arms, straddling their legs so as to seem a complete barrier over the track. It was, Merryl felt, a very foolish, slim little barrier; her heart was in her mouth. The books were all very well when they made these wild statements about animals; it was easy to write such things when you did not have to try and stop a full-grown bull-elephant like Diccon, who had shown that his temper could be tricky. Did Diccon know the rules?

How enormous he looked coming head-on that way! She began to shake; she could not help it.

"Steady on," Teddy whispered between clenched teeth. "Remember we've *got* to get the brute off or there may be a horrible rail smash as a result and we'd never forget that we might have prevented it."

"I won't let go!" Merryl promised and wondered what it would feel like if Diccon did not stop. He was within a couple of yards now and he had not slackened his speed by so much as a second. He curled his trunk over his head in a huge soft 'ess', opened the red triangular cavern of his mouth and roared at them.

"You get off," Teddy cried in defiance, but against the elephant's fine volume of sound his voice was like a little wind sighing in the reeds.

"Stop, Diccon!" Teddy cried, and Merryl shut her eyes, but her clasp never loosened; indeed she gripped so hard that Teddy said long afterwards that her fingers felt like steel. The world seemed to be swinging and rocking about her, strange noises filled her ears, and she wondered if she were going to faint. No, no, not that! She must stay on her feet. How hot the sun was on her neck! How still everything seemed all at once!

She opened her eyes. Diccon was standing right over them, puffing slightly, his trunk curling and twisting, his big head aslant. They had won! In the moral ascendancy of the moment, there was now a rasp of command in Teddy's voice which even the self-willed Diccon recognised.

"Now you come with us!" The boy slapped the elephant's off-leg and pushed slightly, and Diccon obeyed slowly as if bewildered and wondering how the situation he had had so nicely in hand had changed so completely. But he followed meekly enough, and they got him up into a meadow where some drowsy cows looked at them curiously, their jaws moving with the mystery of perpetual motion.

A dull clanking and knocking grew on the summer air, a monotonous sound swelling and throbbing. Round a hidden bend ahead chuffed an old locomotive pulling a long string of box-cars and some cement-trucks. Though the goods-train seemed to be moving lazily enough, it was travelling at a good speed, and if Diccon had been on the line there would have been a disaster. Catastrophe avoided by so slight a margin made the two feel as if a cold weight were resting on their tummies. In all those miles still to go, could they be sure they would always avoid catastrophe?

All that long day they tramped along till their feet felt like warm cushions stuffed into their shoes. At first Diccon was subdued and obedient, but after his evening meal his spirits began to rise again. He trumpeted happily to himself and suddenly curled down his trunk and offered Merryl a ride. She could not have believed that it could feel so glorious to be off her feet, and when Diccon curled his trunk for Teddy too the boy accepted joyfully and was flung aloft. At this rate, for the elephant seemed as fresh as ever, they felt it would be foolish to call a halt.

The sun sank and a moon came up slowly over the evening world, edging with silver the outlines of the puffy little cloudlets. So on through the early night Diccon shuffled till they came to a wide cross-roads. Teddy, who was expecting this, for he had his pocket-map out, pointed the way to Merryl.

"We turn left here, see? I say, Merry, we're half-way home! What *will* they all say to Diccon?"

But Merryl could only shake her head sleepily. All at once she shocked awake. The elephant had stopped and was standing in what they called his listening attitude, head up, trunk curled on his forehead, ears wig-wagging to stand out on each side of his head.

"What does he hear or smell?" Teddy asked uncomfortably. "Get on, do!"

Diccon lowered his trunk and moved off, but it was to the right.

"Oh, no, you don't!" Teddy kicked with his heels on the skull under him, but he might just as well have kicked a granite doorsill for all the notice he got.

"No, Diccon, *please*," Merryl beseeched, for she felt at the end of her tether at last. "Not that way— that's back to the north!" She slipped to the ground, followed by Teddy, weary though they were. They slapped and thumped, pushed and pulled, but Diccon had made up his mind. They seemed to be doomed for ever to wander up and down the dales and roads of England at the sweet mercy of an obstinate young elephant. Oh, why had Great-uncle Bob gone off like that?

Over the low bushes ahead were the twinkling lights of a vast caravan encampment. Borne on the air was the sound of elephants trumpeting at their pickets. Vans and lion-cars on wheels, trucks of props, and trucks loaded with plank seats, and the folded mass of the big top showed where a big circus had camped for the night. Seals were snapping and barking hoarsely; the low evening song of the lions mingled with the sounds of the circus camp.

"Ted, you know, he *is* really clever," Merryl said in admiration. "He must have heard those elephants miles away down the road when the sound was too thin and high for us!"

Down to the camp Diccon stalked, and at his appearance men ran out and stared and shouted. They swarmed round the two children asking questions and gesticulating excitedly as the elephant walked off and joined the other beasts in a long line, where he began helping himself to some of their supper.

"Diccon, you mustn't steal," Merryl cried, blushing hotly for their pet.

But a big bronzed fellow with curly hair white as deal shavings slapped her on the shoulder. "Little lady, as long as Joe Black's Circus has a bale of hay or a crust to spare, ye're all welcome! That's a magnificent beast. You're not selling, I suppose? But come in, come your ways in. Little Salani will see to the elephants!" He looked with curiosity and admiration at the two, for he was not used to children piloting big elephants about the country, even in the circus trade. He shouted to a slim boy with the golden skin of a Ceylon native to look after Diccon.

He took them into his caravan, and Merryl could hardly believe her eyes. A few minutes before there had been nothing round them but the lonely wildness of the countryside at night; their spirits had been in the dumps, their courage and patience exhausted. And now, because of Joe Black's kind invitation, they were in warmth and brightness, with merry faces smiling and eager voices talking. Joe's wife and two sons were the jolliest people, and Joe called for supper loudly, rubbing his huge hands and laughing so boisterously that they must join in.

"Oh, I say, sir and ma'am!" Teddy gasped as they sat down in front of a plateful of food. But they would have no thanks, only insisted on a tale of the children's adventures, for to those who travel the road each newcomer is a source of new stories.

"When we come your way, I send you tickets for the show, yes," Joe Black cried. "You two have got guts, I must say. I don't think at your age I should have done what you have."

"Oh, but he's a darling, is Diccon; truly he is," Merryl cried warmly. "He's only awkward when he wants his own way."

Joe smiled secretly, but one of the animal-trainers looked sober.

"Queer cattle, queer cattle," he said.

Mrs. Black made up a bed for the girl in the spare caravan, and Teddy had the glorious experience of bedding down with the lion-trainer, and they talked far into the night.

In the morning, Joe called to Salani and told him to *settle that elephant's hash*! And Salani whispered in Diccon's ear a long sentence at which the beast appeared surprised.

"Ye'll be all right now," Joe grinned. "You see, there is a language called the elephants' language, and, strange though it is, the people of Ceylon know it and can talk to the elephants, or so they claim. I have seen enough in my time to know that it is true! Salani has told Diccon to obey you as someone perhaps told him long ago to obey your great-uncle."

They looked at the elephant, and he said *grumph-grumph* in his throat and offered them both rides. So up they went, and he marched off with them, while the circus folk stood outside their caravans and waved and cheered in their happy, hearty way.

"Thank you, oh, thank you!" Merryl and Teddy called, and then they were out of sight. And Diccon! What a change! His expression of irritation had vanished. They might have been Rajah and Princess travelling the roads of India. Humbly he obeyed their slightest wish, followed their pointing fingers and stopped and started when asked. He trundled south with them mile after mile, foot-sore but uncomplaining. He went without meals when there was no food and he never stopped for wind or rain or heat.

He landed with them safe and sound at Bramble Cottage and was even going to march right up the path, but Merryl, fearing for Miss Penny's geraniums, shrieked a warning just in time. At the sound of her voice her aunt came running out and came near to having a fit in the porch when she saw what they had brought.

"This is Diccon!" Merryl cried. "It's going to be a smashing zoo, don't you think?"

CHAPTER 4

THE GREAT DAY

"*IS* IT true?" Dodie screamed as she raced up to Bramble Cottage that afternoon. "Teddy said and said about it, but I can't believe—an elephant!"

Merryl, who had washed off the dust and grime and was her old sweet fresh self, laughed wickedly. "Come on and see," she said as Ken and Milly rushed up. "I'm just taking Marcus to introduce him!"

At sight of his friends, the ape leered and jabbered, extending one long hairy arm graciously so that Dodie could take the other hand. A royal prince bestowing the favours of a handshake on a commoner could not have been more condescending.

They went into the little yard. Diccon filled it almost completely, for he stood ten feet high and weighed something like five tons. He raised his trunk in salute to them and something like interest lit up in his small eyes at sight of a brother animal. Not so Marcus. The ape's jaw fell open and he gave vent to some miserable little grunts of jealous disillusionment. That the children, his adored

children, should have another pet beside himself
was almost more than he could bear. His eyes
darkened with some emotion that made his face
appear quite evil. The sloping dome of his head
seemed to move as he wrinkled his brows, and all
the time he muttered. But an expression of deep
cunning dawned in his eyes, and, as if he were
clever enough not to betray himself, one black
leathery hand went up to shield his face.

"Look out, Merry, you'll have to watch Marcus,"
Teddy warned. But in the thrill of patting and
admiring Diccon, his words went almost unheeded.

It was the sight of Miss Penny's worried face
next morning that made Merryl decide that they
must rush on the work of getting Summerleyton—
the name of the secret garden—ready for the zoo.
The words on the sundial kept reproaching her:
Time is precious, so use it wisely.

"Diccon is *sweet*," Aunt Penny tried to explain.
"He's as obedient as can be, but I never know where
his trunk is and today when I was in the scullery
it came sneaking through the window just in front
of my face and felt about as if looking for something.
I declare I nearly dropped the best teapot that I won
on the pier at Brighton as a girl!"

"I *am* sorry," Merryl cried, though it was difficult
not to laugh at the picture. As soon as she could
get ready she rushed over to the secret garden and
stood amazed.

"My stars!" she breathed. "How you have worked!"

The gang stood and smiled at her with conscious pride. They still looked tired from a week's work; their hands were sore and blacked with toil and soil—she had noticed that yesterday—but their eyes shone. Milly's hands were the worst. She had three fingers in sticking plaster and she drooped from the reaction to unaccustomed physical exercise.

But where once had been a dense jungle of grass and weeds was now a flat sweep of ground, the stubble scythed so evenly that walking was as easy as if it had been mown. In the centre the sundial stood up proudly. On the south and west against the high wall were lean-tos, comfortable and dry and heaped inside with hay and straw.

"At this rate," Merryl said, overjoyed, "we can fix the opening date. When shall it be?"

"Saturday?" Milly suggested, sucking a sore finger.

"Okay. All agreed?" Merryl asked, and the motion was carried. She left the others to go into a huddle with the treasurer about the entrance fee and sat down to write an advertisement. "Opening on Saturday, Flaxstead Private Zoo. Admission one penny. Strange animals housed for a small fee!"

"That ought to fetch 'em," Teddy grinned. "What about refreshments, you know? Could we get Tony Trimmer to bring his tricycle and sell his ices?"

"Try it," Dodie said cheerfully. "Granny Gubbins can bake us some of her smashing cheese-tarts. There's enough in the funds to pay her and we'll have lemonade."

"Then you won't," the treasurer said hollowly. "Can't afford lemonade."

"Then we'll make it ourselves," the president finished crisply. "We'll soon get a move on. And we shall have to take it in turns to stay here all day once the zoo is open. We'll split up the work!"

"I could do you meringues," Milly offered surprisingly. "I'm awful good at them."

"Splendid!" Merryl cried enthusiastically, and Rupert began to bark with hysterical joy. It was evident that he knew the word meringue. "I'll make the lemonade, Dodie shall be responsible for the tarts and bringing them here. Ken, what can Ken do?"

"I can't bake for nuts," Ken said hastily, so he was dispatched into Flaxstead with the ad. for the local paper.

Merryl hurried home and as she went she reflected that she was working much harder than she had ever done in any holiday before. If this had been some task set by well-meaning grown-ups how she would have loathed it! When she got back, she took Diccon his lunch and then ran upstairs to tidy her hair. Miss Penny called her.

"Aren't you going to give the elephant his food, dear?" she said from out the cloud of steam as she dished up the Irish stew.

"I have," Merryl answered in amazement.

"Well, he's still hungry and he hasn't a thing before him, poor fellow."

The girl dashed to the back door and there was Diccon swaying at his pickets, blowing gently through his nose in a dolorous little way he had when he was hungry. Not a scrap of his lunch remained on the stones at his feet. Merryl was stupefied and also frightened. Diccon was going to be far too expensive unless the gate-money taken when the zoo opened was more than they expected at present. But she was too tender-hearted not to risk overfeeding the elephant. She got him a further supply of cabbage and sweet hay and stood watching him bolt it as if he were famished. During the next day or two she noticed the same thing happened and at last was driven to watching, for Diccon actually seemed to be getting thinner, and an anxious careworn look in his poor patient face went to her heart. A faint suspicion of the truth made her hide behind the cellar door and watch.

Diccon had just been served with his supper, and she could almost fancy he was eating it in furtive haste, glancing about uneasily with his little eyes full of fear. A faint shuffle from the direction of the toolshed made her turn her head, and then she almost fell down the cellar steps.

Marcus had possessed himself of a large rake which he was half carrying, half dragging, the handle tucked under his arm. His swift advance on his bow legs, his large lips jabbering soundlessly in his excitement, and a comical air of astute defiance on his black face, showed that this was not the first time he had acted thus. Jumping softly up and down, Marcus waved his rake and then, lunging swiftly as a flash of black light, he hooked the greater portion of the elephant's supper out of reach. Diccon slammed out with his trunk in a vain attempt to catch the deceitful ape and it would have gone very hard with Marcus if Diccon had succeeded. But the ape was too quick. Merryl, open-mouthed, watched him, her heart torn with pity at the thought of the short commons poor Diccon had been receiving when she had thought he was unduly greedy.

"I'll watch and see where that imp puts the stuff," she resolved, and saw the heartless ape stuffing the elephant's supper into the compost bin, where, of course, she had never looked. Poor Diccon was swaying again, making his pathetic little noises. She fed him again and then looked round for the culprit. This was a case for hard measures. She went in and got her hairbrush.

"Marcus," she called, and he came at once, a bland smile on his face, and so sweetly innocent was its expression that if she had not seen for herself she could not have believed such a tale of the ape. As it was, she knew she must harden her heart. She sat down on an upturned bucket and in full sight of Diccon took Marcus across her knee.

"It's only fair he should see you punished," she said seriously, and brought the hairbrush down. Merryl was strong, and since coming to live at Flaxstead her muscles had improved. Marcus knew he was in for it and with instinctive cunning he also knew that the more noise he made the more likely it was that his punishment would cease. So he howled his heartbreak to the skies and Miss Penny came out and remonstrated.

"And I wouldn't be that ape," she said when Merryl had explained. "I read somewhere that an elephant never forgets. He'll brood on it for years, but sometime he'll get even!"

The Friday before opening day, Merryl made the lemonade, which she did by the bucketful. She took it across to Summerleyton in the evening, and Marcus, looking extremely sulky, went with her. He was quite used to walking along with people now and they did not have to lead him about, although he was always fastened up in the secret garden. They were met by Milly in a state of great excitement.

"The ad. is in the paper," she screamed. "When

are you bringing Diccon over? It's so thrilling. I've been on duty for today and there are two more animals come—a Nubian goat from Little Bindon Hall and a Belgian hare."

They rushed off together to inspect the newcomers and forgot to tie up the ape—which was a pity, for, when they returned, he had his black face down in one of the buckets and was sucking up lemonade at a furious rate.

"The little beast!" Milly cried in tears. "And, oh, he's had three of the meringues! Look, here's the empty paper cases."

They made a concerted dive at the ape, but he doubled past them and got away.

"We shall just have to be more careful," Merryl said contritely. "Look; we can make up the level of the lemonade again with plain water."

"But that doesn't help my meringues," Milly observed sulkily.

Opening day came at last and even Miss Penny was in a twitter. Diccon was groomed at five o'clock that morning, for Merryl was up at four doing last things. They set off for Summerleyton together, locking up Bramble Cottage. The elephant very gallantly offered the good aunt a ride on his neck, but she flinched away with such an expression of lively horror that he withdrew his trunk hurriedly, looking as abashed as a man does when he has offered his place in a bus and a vinegary spinster has 'lorgnetted' him in refusal. Marcus no doubt could have ridden, but he was wise and kept well away from Diccon's trunk.

When the ape, elephant, Nubian goat and Belgian hare were in their places, and the prize-winning Rupert had been tied up next to a glass case containing the cup he had won, they all felt that the day had begun well.

The original place where the wall had collapsed had been widened and the ground flattened to make an imposing entrance. Ken's clever fingers had contrived a handsome wooden gate.

There was a brush of wheels on the road, and Merryl and Teddy ran to look.

"Heavens, it's Lady Morden's car," Teddy said. "She's a big noise in the county. Who'd have thought she'd recognise local talent?"

A vast woman whose moon face beamed with good nature was helped out by the chauffeur and stood a moment, her wraps undulating round her. She saw the children and advanced.

"*Too* enterprising of you," she cooed at them. "Smithers, get out Uff-guff and carry him carefully. My dears, you simply *must* make a home for Uff-guff. I've no time such as I used to have and he *pines*. So now I will simply *rush* round your *dear* little zoo, and then positively I must *fly*!"

Overwhelmed, they led her in, while Smithers staggered along with a wooden case out of which the most extraordinary noises were coming. Miss Penny, who was rather a moral coward in some things, hid shamelessly. Teddy, marking her defection, winked at her.

"An elephant?" exclaimed Lady Morden. "But this is *wonderful*! I had *no* idea! I must get my cousins out in the wilds to send you stuff. Let me see, you are Merryl Penny. I saw you in your aunt's pew on Sunday, and this is Teddy Carter. Well, I *do* congratulate you, children. Now I'm going. You *will* take care of Uff-guff and see that he has a good tea?"

"Thank you for coming, Lady Morden," Merryl remembered her manners to say, but she was too overawed to ask for gate-money. Ken, however, was made of sterner stuff. He held out his hand.

"That'll be a penny entrance fee," he said, smiling sweetly at her.

"Oh, dear me, yes," Lady Morden cried, looking rather taken aback. She hitched forward an expensive lizard-skin bag hanging on her arm and snapped it open. Ken, trying to see inside, decided that ten shillings at least should be forthcoming from such an ornate piece of work. Lady Morden extracted ninepence and gave it to him with a charming smile.

"For myself, Smithers, and Uff-guff," she cooed. "Now you mustn't say a *word* about its being more than is due!"

"I won't," Ken gasped. The car rolled away in a smother of dust.

"Come on; let's have a look at Uff-guff," Teddy yelled breathlessly, for at sight of Ken's face the gang had collapsed in helpless laughter. They tottered across to the box and prised off the lid. Then once more they went down before gales of mirth.

From the midst of a loud smell of decayed fish looked out the peculiar head and brilliantly marked feathering of a king penguin. He moved his flippers in silly little jerks as if he were waving to them to get him out of his prison. His awful resemblance to Lady Morden flapping at her wraps made Milly roll on the grass, hysterical with giggles.

"What a good thing there's an ornamental pond with fish in it," Teddy said. "I believe those fellows need about twenty haddocks a day!" He looked very grave all at once, remembering the offer to the distant relations to 'send them stuff'. What might not arrive, from king cobras to baboons?

A sharp ping-ping from a tricycle bell announced that Tony Trimmer had arrived with the ices and about twenty children. Merryl was marshalling them to go the rounds when she noticed that Marcus was nowhere to be seen.

"Bother that ape," she said.

Her aunt, who was now returning to the cottage, said she would look out for him, and took her departure. Teddy was just taking the entrance fee from a youngish-old man who had come down the road. Merryl liked the look of him at once. Years afterwards, when they were all firm friends and he was the gang's most devoted slave, he said that he had felt the same interest from the moment he saw them all in the grounds of Summerleyton House. He was about the same age-group as Aunt Penny, which was about fortyish, and he reminded Merryl of Gary Cooper in a tall, lean way. His grey eyes twinkled at her.

"I'm a reporter from the *Flaxstead Chronicle*. They sent me along to write up this."

"Oh, then, you come in free," Teddy said hastily, tendering back the copper. "I know the Press is never charged."

"You keep it," the man said. "I don't suppose this is done for nothing. My name's Naylor, John Naylor."

Merryl introduced them all and then took him round. The day was beginning to be rather exciting. Groups of people were coming in now, and they were not all children, for the twelve bus from Flaxstead had just passed. No one seemed to think that a penny was too much to pay to see an elephant, a goat, a prize terrier, a Belgian hare, and a real king penguin. But Marcus had disappeared.

No one had time to think of lunch; none of the gang could have believed that keeping a zoo would

be such a full-time job. The children had discovered that Diccon would give rides, and Teddy as
treasurer did a few moments' rapid calculation and
then announced that rides were a halfpenny each,
at which no one quailed for an instant. Several
irrepressible infants had twopennyworth each. It
was about three o'clock in the afternoon that Merryl
began to feel absolutely whacked. Excitement and
hard work had made her feel wringing wet; her
damp curls were all stuck to her forehead. The
grounds were full of people. The elephant was having a well-earned rest near one of the lean-tos
where the lemonade was being sold. The penguin
on being released over the pond had retired to the
island in the middle, where he now stood bolt
upright waving his flippers at the admiring crowd.

"Oh, look at Diccon!" Merryl cried in an agony
of horror. His long trunk had come snaking round
the corner just as Miss Penny said it had into the
scullery; only this time he found what he was
seeking: fluid! There was at least three shillings-
worth of lemonade in the end bucket, or at least
there had been a second before, for now Diccon
had had it all. With a last sobbing *gutter-gutter* of
sound the remaining drops were sucked up.

"Diccon, how *could* you?" Merryl cried in
anguish, and the elephant gazing sideways at her
out of one little eye looked overcome with con-
trition. He swayed on his feet and whisked his little

D

tail, but he did not make any attempt to drink up his trunkful, but stood there curling it gently, as if waiting for something. And at that precise moment Marcus appeared. Diccon's quick eyes, which missed nothing, had seen the ape three minutes ago as he returned via the trees from his unauthorised outing. And the elephant had got ready for him.

Not forgotten nor forgiven were the days of miserable hunger when the jealous little ape had stolen his food and hidden it. At sight of Merryl, Marcus came bounding along, cheerfully oblivious of the fact that she was probably angry with him. He pursed up his rubbery lips into a tube as he did when he was getting ready to kiss someone.

The elephant shot out his trunk and the full blast of lemonade took Marcus in his hairy midriff with such force that he was bowled over and swept against the upright of the lean-to, to which the Nubian goat was tethered. With all his breath knocked clean out of him, and his eyes and mouth choked with sticky fluid, Marcus broke down like the baby he was and began to thump his chest and howl his woes to the sky, while the goat turned itself about and planted a shattering kick in the miserable ape's ribs. Up and up Marcus shot, to land with a loud splash in the ornamental pond. Diccon's revenge was complete!

And that effectually closed the day. People

began moving off as if fearing that matters were getting out of hand, and soon Summerleyton grounds were quiet again. Naylor prepared to go and shook hands all round.

"First class," he said. "This should go into some national daily. Excellent! Never heard of anything like it. But look here, kids, are you going to leave all these beasts here at night? Valuable, you know. I'd have someone on guard, I think. And what of the winter?"

"That's what's worrying me," Merryl agreed wearily, but he smiled at her his nice frank smile that had something bracing about it.

"Won't the owner let you use the stables?" he asked. "Magnificent buildings, all stone and timbering—Jacobean, like the house. Could be heated too."

"Oh, I never knew; it's all locked up," Merryl said. But later she spoke to Teddy about the first matter.

"We'll take turns to sleep here, two and two," he suggested. "These warm nights it will be okay, and that end lean-to is dry and warm. With blankets on the hay it would do."

There and then they tossed for first turn, and Merryl and Milly won it. And so Flaxstead Zoo's opening day drew to a close with cool evening winds and the western sky all flaming in lemon and orse. Merryl set about feeding the animals with the dried hay scythed down by Dodie. Uff-guff seemed to have found enough fish in the pond for his supper. Marcus, sulking, would eat nothing. The sugar in the lemonade had dried his coarse black coat into dismal points horribly sticky to the touch. Out of pity for him, Merryl tried to clean him up with her handkerchief wetted in the pond. Milly went off home to bring supper and blankets for herself and Merryl. She promised to be back as soon as she could, and Teddy, Dodie and Ken said they would cycle home round by Bramble Cottage and let Miss Penny know the latest arrangements. Teddy had balanced 'the books' and found that they were three and sevenpence in the clear even after paying Granny Gubbins for the cheese-tarts. A sense of elation and achievement made them all light-hearted, and if it had not been that Merryl could not help being the least bit worried as to the future she would have been gay as a lark.

The late light grew more golden and peaceful. A few early bats began swooping and flittering about. Far away behind the stately trees, the gaunt outlines of Summerleyton House towered up almost grimly. Sitting there watching Diccon chewing his hay, Merryl found that somehow she was more conscious of the silence brooding over the secret garden than she had ever been by day. Rupert and the prize cup had gone home with Milly, for which she was suddenly rather sorry. She did not know what it was of which she felt instinctively afraid, but there was an intangible something in the air about her as the purple shadows lengthened and lengthened. Little shivers crept up and down her spine. Nine o'clock, and still no Milly.

Against the sky, Diccon's outline stood out quaintly. A brown owl wailed from a tall elm. "O-o-o-h, *no*. Oh—dear me—*no!*" it said over and over, as if warning of some sad happening it had heard tell of. Then there came a sound at which Merryl felt herself turn icy-cold. Her heart began to thud even as she told herself to brace up and be sensible.

A low moaning cry mingled with sobbing echoed softly through the dusk. She had to be very firm with herself. "Don't you be a fathead," she scolded. "There's nothing uncanny about it— someone's in trouble."

Though she longed to stay where she was, she forced herself to get up on shaking knees and go forward into the inky shade of the laurustinus bushes, where fat white night-moths fluttered and thumped softly against her face and hands in their blundering way.

Her heart felt near to coming into her throat and getting in the way of her breathing as a pale figure with an enormous head emerged goblin-like and glided forward, sobbing as it came. It was Milly carrying a huge bundle of blankets on her head, a hamper in the other hand; she was weeping bitterly.

"Oh, what's wrong?" Merryl cried, running forward to help.

"All—boo-hoo—all up!" Milly howled, for she was an only child and had been very much spoilt; she always cried when upset, in spite of her age.

"What's up? Do speak plain and stop sniffling."

"Dad was furious that I'd taken the prize cup, and it isn't to come any more," Milly howled lugubriously. "And—oh, oh, it's much worse—he says he *never* said we could 'squat' here. Those were his words. He said as agent for the owner he couldn't allow it and we're to clear out and then I began [to cry and he said we could just stop till we'd found somewhere else and—oh, oh—we shall have to pay for *that* if we ever did find anywhere else!"

Merryl sat there stunned by this awful news. Just as they had felt so established and comfortable they were to be thrown out. She felt she wanted to join in with Milly's noisy lamenting, but her pride forbade her.

"Shut up, do," she exclaimed, shaking Milly. "Come and help me and we'll make ourselves snug for the night." Sniffing dolorously, Milly rose. They spread their blankets, and then, after a last inspection of the animals with a pocket-torch, they turned in. Merryl could not get to sleep, though

Milly was soon puffing and grunting to herself. She lay awake grieving and worrying at this latest blow to their plans. To lie out under the stars like this was even stranger than that night in the hayfield on their long trek back with Diccon, for then she had got Teddy with her, and however much women try to feel equal to men it cannot be denied that the presence of a male takes a good deal of the feeling of responsibility off female shoulders. The sense that she and Milly were responsible if anything should happen was unnerving. But at last even she dozed off.

She awoke with a shock at what seemed hours later, but when she snapped on the torch and looked at her wrist-watch it was only eleven-thirty. The night wind was blowing coldly on her as if something had passed by and made a draught.

"Pooh!" Merryl said, but she was shivering. She stared out into the darkness, fearful of what she might see. Her hands were cold and damp. She wondered how policemen and night-watchmen ever stood up to their jobs.

Then her heart gave a great bump and then seemed to be trying to make up for its lapse by thundering, so that the noise of it knocked in her ears. She was staring across at Summerleyton House, a black rectangle against the star-spun sky. From window to window a light was passing palely, flickering and then moving on.

"Milly, what on earth's *that*?"

Milly woke up slowly and looked. Then she emitted a piercing shriek, at which Marcus began to babble and bang his chain about. But the two girls wanted comfort themselves and the ape mourned alone. Their eyes bulging with terror, they sat clasped in each other's arms watching that eerie flitting light. Merryl was the first to come to her senses.

"Look here, there's nothing really to be scared of. If there's a light then there's *someone carrying it*. We've got to find out. It may be burglars!"

"What?" Milly shrieked again in a transport of fear. "You're not going to march over there and find out?"

"I am," the other said stoutly, though she was conscious of a wish that one of the boys or even Dodie was with her instead.

"Well, I'm not coming," Milly chattered.

"Okay. Stop here and cheer Marcus up!"

"No!" Milly moaned with the fickleness of fright. "I can't stay here without you. I'll come too!"

Across the great smooth space which Dodie had cut they crept cautiously, the cynically remote stars watching.

"Oh!" Milly cried, her voice hoarse with dread. "Something came up behind me and pulled my hair."

"Nonsense," Merryl said, wishing she felt sure of herself. "Nothing could out here in the open."

"I tell you it did! It hurt ever so!"

"Well, let's hide in the shadow of these bushes and watch!" Merryl advised, but she felt it was very uncanny. Suppose it were a boy playing a trick on them, how could he have got away over those thirty yards of open ground behind them, for they had whirled on the instant that Milly had cried out? They waited for ten minutes, but nothing happened.

"Now see here, I'm going to walk out across that space," Merryl said firmly, "and you watch and if it is a small boy you jolly well catch him and we'll thump the daylight out of him."

It took all the nerve she had to advance alone, but she gritted her teeth together and stepped out. The skin on the back of her neck felt to be crawling, but she would not stop and look round. She was in the centre of the open space and then suddenly, without a sound or hint of warning, someone got hold of her curly mop of hair and gave a vicious tug. Panic made her pulses race, but she forced herself to turn and look, though her instinct bade her run for her life.

The open space was empty of the smallest thing. Not even a mouse moved. She stood trembling. But Milly burst out of the bushes laughing hysterically.

"Merry, what asses we have been. I saw it this

time. It was an owl—that one we kept hearing, I expect. I know—I've read of their doing that: swooping on people's heads from behind, mistaking the moving object for their supper. Of course, the wings of an owl don't make the ghost of a sound, and when we spun round he flew on over our heads and we missed him!"

"Sold—by an owl," Merryl said in disgust. "I was scared sick and now I feel I shall never be so silly again. Come on to the house. There'll be just as good an explanation of that light!"

The great pile of Summerleyton House soon loomed above them, all ivy-covered. The twisted chimneys against the stars had an air as if they were leaning and peering over into the secret garden to see what was going on.

The door before them on to the terrace was flanked by stone pillars, at whose feet rank weeds were clustered, almost thrusting the flags of the terrace apart. Merryl tried the door. It was clammy to the touch, coldly wet with dew, and locked fast. In spite of her good intent, Milly's teeth began to stutter tog ther like a cement-mixer.

"You can't get in; that settles it!"

"No? There's a broken window here. Gimme a leg up on to the ledge, Milly."

"Don't," the girl begged, but she had to do as she was told. Merryl crept in, then turned and held down her hands for her chum, who was so stunned

by the other's audacity that she had lost all power
to resist and was hauled up vigorously into what had
been the long drawing-room overlooking the
terrace. Merryl sniffed.

"Mice," she whispered and flashed her torch
round.

Indescribably beautiful was that old room, with
its tall windows and carved panelling, its hand-
painted ceiling, and the furniture of long ago
shrouded in dusty covers.

"There is something awfully sad about a place
people have loved and lived in," she whispered. "I
wonder what they thought and did. Who worked
those tapestries?"

"I don't care who did," Milly said crossly. "Let's
go upstairs and satisfy you and then go back. The
less I have of this atmosphere, the better!"

But as they went on tiptoe from room to room,
Merryl grew more and more excited. Great stained-
glass windows in the echoing hall, the balustraded
glory of a perfect Carolinian staircase, wide and
shallow-stepped, the soft colours of Pyrenean
marble, all these things held her breathless. Never
had she imagined that Summerleyton House was
like this inside. The folk who had once lived here
had drifted down these same stairs in billowing
crinoline or Napoleonic muslins, and walked and
loved in the wrecked rose-gardens and read the
message on the sundial.

Up the stairs the two crept and found a long gallery of carved oak above the terrace.

"Look, there is a light under that door," Milly squeaked. "I wish I hadn't come!"

"Don't be a goose. I expect it's a reflection or something."

Merryl went boldly across and flung the door wide; and then even she wondered if she were dreaming or no. An ordinary oil-lamp stood on a table covered by modern books of reference and piles of papers. At one side stood an up-to-date typewriter. Seated behind the desk and staring at them open-mouthed was no less a person than John Naylor. He half rose and some of the papers fluttered to the floor. Stupefied, he recognised them.

"It's Merryl and Milly?" he asked.

"What are you doing here?" Merryl asked faintly. "I thought it was all shut up and so when we saw your light——"

"You investigated? I think that was darned plucky!" John Naylor was staring at them with strange admiration in his wide grey eyes.

"We weren't a *bit* frightened really," Milly giggled.

"Well, as you've interrupted work, I'll call it a day and pack up and see you home!"

"But we aren't at home—I mean——" and Merryl explained.

His amazement increased. "Standing guard all night because of what I said? By heck, there's something in the modern kids! Well, look, I'll stand guard with you, eh? That is, if Diccon doesn't object."

"Oh, how lovely! But what are you *doing* here?" Merryl cried, overjoyed at having company and support.

He laughed almost shyly as he put away his papers and tidied the room. "Well, I shall have to trust you two not to tell, you know. I am writing a book about the Naylors of Summerleyton." His tone was rather sad. "I come here nights to work, for the place gives me inspiration, though they say I have no right here. But I belong here. I too am a Naylor!"

"Of course—your name—but I don't see——?"

"I am a distant relation and this house is really mine, but I can't prove it. Somewhere hidden here in this building is the proof, but I have searched in vain." Naylor looked at them smiling and shrugging and Merryl thought again how handsome he was.

"Oh, how thrilling to be trusted—we won't ever tell," Merryl whispered. "Do you think that we might find the proof you want?"

"You might; you never know now that you are here with your zoo!" John Naylor said. "Now come and show me the way to your 'lair' and I'll snug down too. I've kept you up quite late enough as it is!"

"What an end to the opening day," Merryl breathed. "You wouldn't mind our staying here if —if you proved your claim?"

"I'll do more—I'll subsidise the zoo," he laughed.

CHAPTER 5

DICCON'S EXCITING RIDE

FOR THE next few days Merryl and Milly had little time to think much about John Naylor or his remarkable story. Even the threat hanging over the zoo was thrust into the background of importance for the time being. It was Dodie's remark next morning which helped them to forget.

"Uff-guff's eaten all the goldfish in that pond!" she said in an awed whisper. "I feel quite guilty about it; there were some beauties, some about six inches long, and they're worth quids now."

Teddy took a completely commonsense view.

"Well, he's *had* them; you can't get them back by worrying. Quit looking like a wet week-end."

Ken hurried up. They were all grooming and feeding the animals. Their sleeves were rolled up and they had on aprons, even the boys.

"Oh, I say," he began. "Uff-guff's eaten all the fish."

Teddy put down the mop with which he was washing Diccon's face.

"Here's another Jeremiah! What of it, son? If you think the zoo funds run to restoring damage done, you're in for a disappointment."

"It's not that," Ken explained hurriedly. The boy had constituted himself especially the penguin's nursemaid. "Uff-guff's hungry. He is making the most pathetic signs and flipping his flippers, if you follow me."

"Look in that hamper," Merryl laughed. "Aunt Penny sent some herrings over last night. The boy had brought her too many. He might like those."

"He certainly might," Ken agreed and went off with them. Five minutes later he was back. "Look here, Uff-guff won't look at them," he said accusingly, as if their heartlessness in suggesting herrings for his pet hurt him.

"The more fathead he," Dodie replied witheringly, but they all went to look. The latest recruit to the zoo was standing bolt upright on the bank of his little pond; his beak was pointed skywards, and in his gaze was a wild yearning look as if he were working out some abstruse problem of the stars. His flippers moved gently from time to time. At his feet and unregarded lay his silvery breakfast.

"D'you suppose he's ill?" Merryl asked anxiously, but the king penguin appeared in the best of health. He lowered his bill, cocked an eye down at the food, and then gazed in mute appeal at the children.

It was only by the merest chance, later, that they found out what was wrong. They could not know that penguins, being the world's most accomplished swimmers among birds, are so used to catching their dinner while doing the breast stroke, so to speak, that it is an impossibility for them to eat it off the ground. Uff-guff was starving in sight of plenty. They thought he was sulking. They had much to learn.

"Look, if he won't eat it he'll have to learn to," Teddy said. "That's what we did with Molly, our old cat. She got awfully finicky and wouldn't drink milk if we'd skimmed it and Dad said he'd be hanged if he'd let Molly run his farm for him!"

"What happened?" Merryl asked breathlessly, taking her sympathetic gaze off the hungry bird.

"Course she gave in after howling the place down. Now we'll be as sensible as he was and get back to work."

It seemed to be a morning of minor disasters. Marcus was in a fretful mood and demanded attention, pretending that he had a thorn in his foot, an old trick which no longer worked. Milly had brought a worming powder for Rupert, thinking to get some help in administering it.

"Why, it's gone! I put it down just here," she cried, hunting feverishly through the first-aid box, a soapbox containing the animals' simple wants.

"Well, it's gone now," Ken said almost impatiently. "I think the Nubian goat and Rupert are the only two of our pets who never give any trouble. There's Diccon feeling off it now!"

"How do you mean, off it?" Merryl asked in alarm. "He was all right first thing."

"Won't eat his breakfast. Just tossed it over with his trunk and blew at it in a depressed kind of fashion!"

When Merryl examined Diccon she knew that the big beast must be ailing, for there was a lacklustre expression in his eyes. All at once an overwhelming sense of responsibility made her quail. If he were ill what on earth could they do? You couldn't put an elephant to bed with a couple of hot-water bottles. Fancy rubbing that chest with liniment or making him take hot honey and milk or onion gruel! She felt that an older head than hers must decide—the vet.

"Ken," she called, "you've got your bike here; can you go for Mr. Plimmer? I don't like the look in Diccon's eye."

"Can he look at Uff-guff while he's here?" Ken bargained. "You know he'll charge for the visit!"

"Ask the treasurer if the funds'll stand it," Merryl cried desperately, but arguing that it would be cheaper than a new elephant. Ken sped away. Merryl felt that she knew now exactly how a mother feels, because at that precise second a piercing screaming broke out near the sundial.

"Heavens, what now?" she thought, and ran.

Marcus was standing with both long hairy arms wrapped about the stone leg of the sundial, pressing the coldness of it against his black stomach, which certainly looked alarmingly distended. He was rolling his eyes, his rubbery lips were writhed back to show his fangs, and he howled, his wrinkled brows working as if he were beside himself.

"Oh, Marcus, what is it?" She almost wept at sight of such pain. At the sound of her voice the miserable Marcus flung himself away from the stone and rushed to her, winding his arms about her knees and looking up into her face with imploring eyes. His shrieks redoubled.

She kneeled on the grass to come down to his level and felt his bloated tummy tenderly. At her first gentle prod he screamed and gibbered and fairly danced upon his bowed legs.

"Oh—I know!" she cried, enlightenment flooding her, and intense relief with it. "You greedy little wretch; you took poor Rupert's worming powder and now it's getting you. Serves you jolly well right!"

Such a glance of stricken anguish lighted the ape's trembling face at this condemnation that her heart reproached her and she hastened to offer comfort. But he pushed her off to flee bounding over the grass like a sooty imp from the nether regions, his shadow leaping and gesticulating with him. He reached the elms and fled aloft like a hunted thing. Out along a branch he leaped and then flung himself off it, but saved what looked like deliberate suicide by holding on with two feet and one hand so that he was suspended head down. In that position he was violently sick and Merryl was thankful.

"He won't thieve things again in a hurry," she said to Teddy. "Look, as the health standard seems a bit off today what about putting a notice on the gate that the zoo is closed?"

"Splendid," the boy agreed and raced off to do it. Milly and Ken hurried up at that moment with Dodie and John Naylor.

"It would have taken ages getting the vet," Ken explained. "We met Mr. Naylor outside and he says he's been two years in India and understands elephants, so——"

The big lean man smiled down at them, especially at Merryl and Milly, with all the pleasant interest of a secret shared. Then he turned briskly about, deposited his coat on a box, rolled up his shirt-sleeves and demanded to see his patient. They had no doubts at all as to his knowledge and skill when they saw the way he examined Diccon, who was curling his trunk up and down in a hopeless kind of way. He had stopped rocking on his feet, and healthy elephants usually rock most of the time.

"Hum," John Naylor said with his cheery grin. "What this fellow needs is work! You say he came off a farm? Well, I bet he worked on it too and he's missing the regular exercise."

"What about our place, eh?" Teddy cried in huge delight, for he saw possibilities in the matter. Only yesterday, Mr. Carter had hinted that enor-mous quantities of hay and roots were being diverted to the zoo. But if he were to get cheap labour more powerful than his biggest tractor, well, that quite altered things.

"Now, where do I get what I need?" asked Naylor.

"Aunt Penny's not far off," Merryl said, so Naylor was dispatched with Dodie as guide to obtain what he needed for the elephant.

Merryl went and had another mournful look at Uff-guff. "These children of ours," she sighed, for the king penquin was still making pathetic movements with his flippers, while into his eyes had crept a despairing look. She saw in a new light his long stiff body and awkward thick neck and all at once she solved the bird's problem.

"You poor thing!" she said in acute remorse. "And we thought you were sulking, when you couldn't reach your breakfast at all." She picked up a slippery herring by its tail, the scales slipping off as she grasped it, to lay like sequins on her print frock. She dangled it invitingly against Uff-guff's beak.

There was a gobbling snatch and the herring was gone; Merryl almost thought for a moment that her fingers had gone too. Uff-guff was famished! Before either had really recovered breath, the herrings were all gone and the bird was peering about in a disappointed way as if he felt that he had only just begun. One more problem was solved and that was that penguins have to be fed by hand.

It was exciting, a little frightening at times, to think of all that they must learn, but it was the most engrossing play that any of them had ever experienced.

Dodie and Naylor came back after a while and Dodie said aside to Merryl, and rather crossly, that they'd have been back ages ago if he had not been so taken with Bramble Cottage and gone all over it with Aunt Penny, after which that misguided creature had offered him a glass of her raisin wine and he'd had it.

Something for Diccon was wrapped in a cabbage-leaf and looked enormous.

"Now then, come on, Diccon," Naylor said in his hearty way, and tended it. Diccon rolled his little eye round and looked at it in lively horror. He curled his trunk with a violent flicking sound up out of harm's way, opened a triangular red mouth and said: "*Phrumph-umph-umph!*" His tones were so determined and shrill and so exactly said 'certainly not' that the dullest mind must have understood.

"M-m, that's a pity," Naylor mused. "Taken against it from the start. He's too big to hold his nose and give it him by force, and yet he must have it. Come on, Diccon, it's lovely. Look, all cabbage."

"Phrumph! That's just what it ain't," Diccon replied, and he sidled away, his picket-chains clanking.

"I wonder if one of you tried——" Naylor suggested seriously.

"Let me," Merryl begged and took the heavy thing in her hands. She glanced round for inspiration, but saw only that ring of anxious faces, for the elephant was a tremendous favourite. Marcus had descended his tree and was now sitting limply on the grass, shivering and dejected, making the most of a patch of hot sunshine, trembling fingers plucking at his lips.

In her pocket that morning Merryl had brought a bar of chocolate for the ape, but subsequent events had made her forget.

"I'm going to try guile," she whispered. "Play up to me!" Then aloud: "All right, Diccon, if you won't have this lovely pill someone shall have it that likes it." She walked slowly away.

Diccon, like many another male, had been enjoying the flattering interest he was causing and, like the spoilt baby he was, had been deliberately refusing the cabbage in order to prolong the fuss. So cunning are even the best of pets! He'd no objection to tasting mixtures in cabbage leaves— rather liked them, bless you!

He still hated Marcus with the cold deadly hatred of all elephants for something which has taunted or misused them. His eyes fairly goggled when Merryl walked off towards Marcus. All the little crowd about him melted as the gang followed her.

"Come and have this," she called to the ape. Her back was to Diccon, so that he did not see that she was proffering the chocolate. Marcus stopped shivering and rubbed his watering mouth. He began to chatter in his old friendly way, held his arms over his head and waved his hands, flapping from the wrists, in the true ape salute.

"This'll taste better than worm powders," Merryl told him loudly. She could have danced as an outraged *phrumph* from Diccon told of his disgust at her lack of perception. Marcus reached out for the chocolate, but she went close up to him so that the elephant should not see what he was getting.

There was a dolorous trumpeting from Diccon, who repented of his waywardness. That settled it. They had won! Merryl gave the cabbage to him and he fairly grabbed it with his trunk and shot it into his mouth; he gave a couple of circular chews of his enormous jaws and it was gone. A pleased expression on his face made him appear positively genial, for no doubt the big pachyderm considered that he had done the ape out of a *bonne-bouche*.

John Naylor laughed. "I don't think you need me," he said. "You seem perfectly well able to cope!" And he took himself off.

For the next day or two nothing much occurred, but, as Merryl pointed out, that mostly meant with them that something was due to break loose. And it did. The thing began with Diccon's taking on farm work.

As the zoo was visited by strangers mostly in the

afternoon, it was arranged that the elephant should
work from seven a.m. till one o'clock. Mr. Carter
was so delighted that he broadcast Diccon's fame
and that of the zoo far and wide, so that a farmer
from the other side of the country rang up and
asked Merryl if she would like a two-headed calf.
She refused, shuddering.

Teddy took Diccon to and from his work and
sometimes Ken went too, but never Ken or Dodie
alone, for they had never felt quite so at home with
the elephant as Teddy and Merryl, who had brought
him on that long trek down from Yorkshire.

It was a week later that Teddy asked Merryl if
any new arrival had come to the zoo during the
morning. She said no. "There was a note from
Lady Morden to say that Uff-guff had to be hand-
fed. She'd forgotten to mention it! Really, some
people are the limit. Fancy waiting till now.
Scatterbrained old thing. He'd have been dead by
now if we hadn't used our brains. Why did you
ask about new arrivals?"

"Because a big red-painted wooden van thing
built on to a lorry passed the farm coming in this
direction and it just shouted animal transport."

"Well, it hasn't turned up here! Now look sharp,
Teddy, and help me before we open for the after-
noon. There's your lunch over there, and Aunt
Penny put in some of your favourite apricot-tart.
I must go and feed Uff-guff."

Two days later, Merryl happened to be at home when lunch-time came. She had gone to collect the penguin's fish and to get her own food. She was just leaving when the telephone shrilled at her and she picked up the receiver.

"Oh, Teddy, it's you!" she cried in some surprise. "Where are you—at Granny Gubbins's? What's the matter?"

Thinly Teddy's voice came back, and in it was a note of stricken fear as at some dire catastrophe.

"Yes, only place I could think of to phone from; hoped to catch you before you left. I was walking Diccon back when that big red van thrust out from a side road, where it must have been *hiding*. Two men got out, proper thugs—I see that now! They offered me and Diccon a lift. Said they were a firm of carters who often took animals and that they'd handled elephants. Like an idiot I accepted, as it was hot as fire and three miles still to go. I helped them box him—I could kick myself blue—and then just as I was getting in they knocked me down in the road and drove off. I'd no time to take the number!"

"Oh, Teddy, how *frightful*! Oh, what shall we do? What do you want me to do?"

"Slip down on to the Summerleyton road," Teddy panted, "and if they pass, take the number. Not that it helps much. If they are real crooks they can change it."

Merryl slammed down the receiver and fled. She had only a short distance to go and all the time her mind was whirling. What good could an elephant be to those men? They could sell it, of course, if they knew of some market where a fine specimen was wanted and no questions asked. Diccon had no distinguishing marks. He would be extremely difficult to trace. She ran like the wind. If only she could be in time!

There was the Summerleyton road and there behind its high wall was the zoo. Coming along to meet her was Dodie, who often did this.

"Marcus is a lamb," she called when she saw Merryl. "He went——" She broke off at sight of her chum's face.

"Never mind the ape. Listen and run as we go!" Her heart pounding, the breath wheezing from her so that it was difficult to talk, Merryl jerked out her story. Dodie's face whitened.

"The beastly, dirty sneak-thieves! What can we do?"

"Get that number if it's the last thing we do. It's our only chance. *Here it comes!*"

Yes, there was no mistaking it—a big heavy lorry, the upper part painted red. It was not driving too fast, no doubt because of its contents. For all that, it was covering the ground. There was nothing suspicious in their standing to look at it as it lumbered past, so they paused to wait till it came abreast, their nerves stretched to snapping point.

"It's slowing up," Dodie gasped, the breath squeaking through her nose.

"Stand firm," Merryl warned. "Don't show what you're thinking on your face."

"I'll try, but I feel *awful*!"

"Hi!" one of the men called as the lorry came to a stop and stood quivering gently with its own pent-up powers. They were a tough-looking pair all right. Their unshaven chins were blue, their faces brick-red. Both wore oil-stained overalls and both were smoking.

"Yes, what is it?" Merryl asked, stepping into the road. Her nerves as usual had stilled in the face of the crisis and she was now as calm as if the lorry and its crew were just a passing taxi with a load of summer visitors.

"Is this the road to Yepperton?" one man asked, pointing.

"Yes," she replied slowly as if thinking. "But you'll have to watch. There's a tricky turn at the bridge. You have to take the smaller road as it's the main!"

"Okay!" There was a churning rumble inside the vehicle, a *churr* and *chug* as it moved off. With stepping into the road to answer, Merryl had done an excellent thing, for now she was close to the lorry. No one could miss reading the number-plates so near as that. It had been an unforeseen stroke of luck that the men should have been uncertain of their way.

Then one of those wild impulses came to Merryl, when she acted first and thought afterwards. As the lorry moved off, she saw her chance. There was a huge tail-board, which could be lowered to form a ramp for taking animals in. This was now chained up over the closed doors of the van part. The chains passed outside the tail-board to fasten to two sturdy ledges, like the 'chains' in an old full-rigger.

Merryl waited for no more but sprang up, grasped the chain with her hands and stood with her feet resting on the ledge. There was a scrambling rush and Dodie was beside her.

"What now?" her chum asked in a scared whisper, fierce with feeling.

"Now we jolly well follow and see where they go. Wish I'd had time to leave a message. Hush, Dodie; don't rattle that chain so; I'm scared they'll hear us, but they never looked round or they couldn't have missed."

The lorry was roaring along now, jouncing and thundering. At one special plunge, when it was taking what seemed like a runaway charge down the hill towards Long Yepperton, a grunt they both knew came from inside.

"Diccon, it's all right," Merryl whispered and was sure he heard and was comforted.

"What'll they say if they see us—I mean the people in the towns?"

"I don't know. If I could be sure they'd believe us I'd yell as soon as I saw a policeman!"

But they did not get the chance. It was soon clear that the men's asking for the town had been solely so that they could avoid it. At the tricky place they zoomed away on the broad road, leaving Yepperton on the right.

"How long, I wonder, can we stand like this?" Merryl thought and cast a glance at Dodie. Pride forbade her to be first to cry off and yet theirs was anything but a comfortable situation. Their hands grew numb with clinging to the chains, their feet were stiff, and their knees like blocks of wood.

But Dodie turned and grinned at her and not a squeak of complaint escaped her. Actually, this was the first big adventure Dodie had ever been in, and it was thrilling her to the roots of her hair.

Those men must have been clever map-readers, for never once did the lorry pass through a town. They had been puzzled by that bit near the bridge and had asked, otherwise they evidently relied on their own judgment.

On and on the lorry thundered.

"They'll stop some time, nearly certain to, for petrol or food or something," Dodie whispered. "Then you know what'll happen. One of them will saunter round to kick all the tyres and check up and then——"

Merry¹ nodded. "And they're slowing right now," she breathed. "Squint out your side, Dodie. I daren't. The driving mirror's this side!"

"Petrol pump half a mile down the road," Dodie reported. "We're sunk!"

"Not on your life! What's the matter with the roof—it's flat?"

It did not seem too difficult, for the framework of the tail-board had heavy cross-pieces to give strength and with these and the chains they managed to scramble up, though it was a perilous swaying journey where one slip would have meant a nasty fall and being left behind.

"Just made it," Dodie exulted as they collapsed on the grimy roof and the lorry halted. "And how we did it with our feet and knees so stiff I don't know."

The men got down, and while one of them saw to the tank being filled, the other, even as they had thought, walked round. With beating hearts they heard him pause for a long while in the rear.

"I say, Jim, come here; there's sand and earth on these ledges!"

Merryl and Dodie clung together in an agony as Jim came to look.

"Aw, I shouldn't worry," he said slowly. "Some kids pinched a ride, likely, when we wasn't looking. Is the animal okay?"

"Reckon so. Let's get a move on. I'll settle with the man."

Once more they were on their way and now the situation was worse, for neither girl dared descend to their old position. It sounded easy enough to say they would lie on the roof, but there was nothing to hold on to and at the curves it was difficult not to be swung off.

Dusk descended and deepened, but just as the two were feeling a trifle more secure they got the worst shock of the whole journey. The van part made the lorry very tall, and already they had suffered much from branches slapping at them. Now Dodie, peering ahead, saw against the egg-shell-blue sky of evening the dark segment of a railway bridge which spanned the road.

"Merry," she cried aghast, "there isn't room! We shall be killed."

Merryl shot one quick look ahead. There was not even time to scramble to the rear and descend to their old place.

"Lie absolutely flat," she hissed. "Lay your head sideways like this, arms out. Now cross your fingers: here it comes!"

Even a three-inch clearance above their heads was enough, but it was a frightful thing to be hurled helplessly towards an arched opening with only that amount of room. Could they have watched it approach, their nerve would have broken, they would have instinctively started away and been caught. But they could not see the horror before them lying as they were.

There was a hollow booming roar and the lorry plunged below the bridge. They both had a dreadful sight of uneven stones, the light flickering over them and so close that their eyes could not focus properly. Then they were out on the other side, their hair full of dust, their hands shaking so that they could scarcely hang on.

"That," Merryl said, "was the nastiest thing that ever happened to *me*. How do you feel?"

"Terrible!" Dodie said, her chin jumping.

Gradually their frayed nerves settled down and calm returned.

"My, I'm hungry!" Merryl said. "I wonder how poor Diccon feels. He's always had his meals so regularly."

"What is the time?"

"Close on eight; they'll surely make a halt for the night?"

"Not necessarily, as there are two of them. One can sleep as the other drives. But you'd think they would stop to have a meal."

"Don't worry," Merryl whispered; "that's just what they are doing."

The men got down. The lorry door slammed. They had chosen an ideal place: a grassy verge to a little-used lesser highway and near dense woods.

There was a chink of metal, and Dodie, taking a cautious peep on her side, reported.

"Sitting on the grass opening a Thermos flask and papers of sandwiches. The sight of them's making me drool. They're chatting away, but you can't hear what they say."

"Dodie, do you realise something?" Merryl hastened to explain. The men, when they stopped the lorry, had backed it on to the grassy verge so that it could be driven straight out again. They were sitting on the left of the machine, the side where the road ran upon which they meant to proceed. "We could get down, sneak round into the cab, and drive Diccon back home again!"

The preposterous daring and colossal cheek of some suggestions are so tremendous that they daze opposition from the start. It is the lukewarm, hesitant plan which begets a storm of counter-suggestions and amendments.

"Of course—yes," Dodie answered firmly. "Why didn't I think of that? Er—can you drive?"

"Yes. My cousin used to let me drive his milk-lorry full of churns from the sheds to the dairy. He taught me gear-changing and how to steer properly. I might crash the gears in until I get used to them, but we'll manage somehow."

"It's against the law," Dodie hazarded, but Merryl shrugged.

"I know it is, but what can we do? It'll lead to

the men being taken up if we can pull it off, and honestly I can't bear to think of poor Diccon in their hands. Even if I have to go to jail for it"— with stormy defiance—"I'm going to try!"

But her courage almost forsook her in the long waiting time while they listened to the men at their meal. Their one hope was that the two would take forty winks over a pipe before resuming their journey. Merryl actually caught herself hoping they would not so it would be taken out of her power to attempt the fearful task she had set herself. The contemplation of this cowardice in her attitude filled her with shame and she was utterly miserable.

Suddenly Dodie grasped her arm. "Lighting up pipes," she whispered. Then, later: "Their smoke is over; they're having a doze. Now for it!"

"Yes," Merryl said hollowly.

They were in full view as they scrambled carefully down over the tail-board; the only hope was that in the soft darkness of night they would be hidden. It felt very strange to be once more on solid ground that did not bounce and rumble under them. Round to the far side they crept and up into the high driving-cab. Merryl, feeling more dead than alive, wedged herself in behind the big wheel. The cab smelt of petrol and rubber. Underfoot the flooring was worn and dusty. They could see the glint of starlit road through chinks in it.

The girl took a swift look round at the controls. "There won't be time looking for anything once we start. Here's the ignition switch, there's the starter-button, and there is the switch for the lights."

"Oh, do hurry!" Dodie almost wailed in an agony at any delay.

Trembling, Merryl turned the switch and pressed the self-starter. The lorry began thundering and shaking gently under its breath, so to speak. Merryl pushed out the clutch and put the lorry into gear. Slowly she let in the clutch and gently pressed the accelerator. There seemed a good deal of banging, but the lorry was moving. She grasped the wheel like grim death. Her knees were so tremulous that she could hardly keep her foot on the accelerator.

"Turn the wheel quickly!" Dodie shrieked. "We're nearly on to the road!"

"It's so heavy," Merryl panted. But she twisted and twisted and could have whooped for joy when the lorry turned obediently and they took the road with a quaking jerk which tested the springs to the uttermost. She let the wheel spin back while she pushed out the clutch again to change to a higher gear. Somehow she crashed it in.

Leaving a track like a drunken S, they boomed up the road.

There was a yell behind them as the two men, startled out of their doze, came pounding along, but though an inexperienced driver sat at the wheel the lorry was going faster than the men could run and they dropped back, shaking their fists and shouting convulsive threats that fortunately the girls could not hear. Merryl put the lorry into top gear.

"And one comfort," Dodie pointed out, "they can't run to a callbox and call the coppers, for it was stolen goods."

"Hope Diccon is feeling okay with all this jouncing?"

"Don't talk," Dodie shrieked; "mind what you are doing!" She fumbled for the lights. There was a snap, and broad beams of golden light wavered ahead, killing the night colours, turning all things to a shade of silver dust.

"That's better," Merryl approved. "Now I can see what I'm doing. Can you remember how far we came on this road?"

"We didn't turn anywhere; I noticed that," Dodie confirmed. "Not till we've passed under that arch again, and then there was a crossroads, but it'll be time enough to worry when we are there."

Heady exultation at their success rose in them so that they wanted to shout and sing, to make whoopee as they drove. Merryl was beginning to think that driving was really nothing to worry about, even though it was difficult to keep a perfectly straight track. But her eyes were already aching from the straining effort she was making to stare ahead and relegate shadows to their proper importance. Twice she swerved dangerously because a dark band of inky shadow ahead looked like a stone wall across the road until the headlights caught and dispersed the fancy. Night-driving is a test even to experienced men.

Then into the lights dashed a silver rabbit. They knew that it was really brown, but it was the same bone-white colour as everything else. It leaped ahead along the road as rabbits will, so petrified with horror of the thundering monster behind it that it could not break off to either side and escape. Why they did not mount the bank, plunge through the hedge, and fall into a field neither of them ever knew.

"I shall run over it—I can't help it." Merryl shivered as the lorry bounded from side to side. With some unexplained perversity, the more terrified she was of slaughtering the rabbit, the faster she drove, until at last, when the bunny dived into the hedge, they were hurtling along at a breathless speed—for them. Merryl took her foot off the accelerator and forced the gear lever into neutral. The lorry slowed and stopped.

"They couldn't catch us now; we're five miles away. I must get out and see if Diccon is okay."

A dreadful thought struck Dodie. "Suppose it isn't Diccon?"

"But we heard him!" Merryl climbed out stiffly, went round and shouted to the animal. He had air-holes, but they were high up on the sides of the van. He heard her, and a delighted squealing *phrumph* came to them.

"You *are* all right?" Merryl asked, and Diccon said he was, but very hungry, thank you. Merryl drove more slowly, trying hard to make less noise with her gear-changing, and when they came to the cross-roads she stopped again so that Dodie could get out and read the signpost.

"Turn left," she said when she came back. "We have all night to get along in. Oh, I could yell when I think how we've outwitted them!"

They were lucky because the country here was very flat; they had met no hills to test their skill. When the early dawn came, Merryl knew she had gone wrong somewhere, for they passed through a big village which neither of them remembered. A couple of policemen outside the station looked at them with some surprise, and their faces grew very thoughtful when they saw the slight figure crouched over the wheel, while a white-faced companion studied an outspread map.

"*This is it!*" Merryl gasped. "Those men gave gave us the meanest kind of look!"

Two miles out of the village they met their first real obstacle. It was a long steep hill rising away before them, the white ribbon of road disappearing over the crest fully two miles away. Merryl set her teeth, jumped on the accelerator, and they took the first long slope with a bang and a roar which shook their very livers, Dodie said.

Then Merryl began to get frightened. Do what she would the power seemed to be going out of the machine. She tried hard to change down to a lower gear to get them over the incline, but the gear would not be forced in. They were getting slower and slower with the imminent risk of stopping and running backwards.

In her panic she felt she must pull up, that at all costs she must get the lorry across the road so that it could not slip. She completely forgot the foot and hand brakes. She swung the wheel in a desperate last attempt for safety. They crashed into the bank, the engine gave a despairing mumble and they were stationary.

She sat white-faced, while Dodie burst out crying. A hoot down the road told of the approaching police bike.

"Na then, what's all this?" the sergeant said, looking at the woebegone two. "You know, I suppose, that you've no right to be in charge of this yer lorry?"

"I know," Merryl gulped. "But it was Diccon!"

"Diccon 'oo?" inquired the man, cocking a doubting eye at them. "I always find, miss, that it's the way to go on, shoving the blame

on to someone else. This Diccon now, brother or
father?"

"Diccon is an elephant!" Merryl replied de-
jectedly.

The policeman started and looked at her as if he
thought she must be very simple indeed. "I
dessay," he said shortly. "And I expect the kangaroo told yer to do it and the lions egged you on."

"Don't be silly," Merryl said, recovering. "Diccon's in this van. Oh, Diccon!" she raised her
voice.

"*Phrumph-phrumph*," the elephant trumpeted hun-
grily.

"Strike me pink!" Robert muttered, passing one
hand over his forehead. "Now look 'ere, young 'uns,
you'd better come clean." So they came clean.

It took the man some time to unravel the whole
of the tale, and if he had not been a policeman
Merryl would have said that a look of incredulous
admiration warmed his face. But he was a policeman, so it must have been fancy. He turned the
lorry on to the road again, slung his bike up
behind, and drove them into a nearby town, where
he helped them make a full and detailed report.

"That's all right," the officer in charge affirmed.
"We've been told to look out for this van. The
elephant was stolen from the Flaxstead Private
Zoo and we can return it. You are being let off
with a caution," he told the two, "but we would

like a word with your people. The van must come back, so that we can trace the thieves. You can see to it, sergeant."

"Oh, please, first," Merryl pleaded, "can poor Diccon have some breakfast? He must be famished!"

"What about yourselves?"

"Oh, we don't care," Dodie said chirpily in her relief.

The sergeant's wife, however, took them to her quarters and gave them some hot food and when they came back they found a strange scene. The van rear doors were open and Diccon, who had somehow managed to turn round inside, was facing outwards, trumpeting shrilly and waving his trunk about. Crockery lay everywhere smashed to smithereens. As the girls ran out into the yard a porridge plate came hurtling to smack into atoms against a brick wall. Three policemen, very red in the face, were arguing angrily.

"So sorry, miss," one of them said, "but 'e won't look at 'is breakfast and it's come crool on the station crockery. The only thing what 'e's consented to eat was a happle."

"What did you give him?" Merryl quavered, while Dodie collapsed helplessly laughing.

"Bit of nice grilled bacon, but he didn't seem to fancy it and he put his foot in his tea and you see where the porridge goed!"

It was sliding stickily down the wall.

"Hay or some cabbages," Merryl suggested weakly.

"Hay? Like a blooming 'orse?" one of the men cried. "Well, miss, I must say, miss, you do surprise me."

On the drive home their nice sergeant became great friends with them and they found his name was Sid Jones, that he was married and had a boy about Dodie's age. But he remained sceptical about the zoo. Dodie and Merryl fairly lived for the moment when they could convince him. About two that afternoon the van turned into the grounds of Summerleyton House and came to a stop. There was a shriek of joyous welcome as the gang swarmed about them, but the most bewildered person was the sergeant.

Uff-guff had waddled over the grass in the wake of Milly, who had been feeding him, and now stood waving his flippers for attention. The Nubian goat tripped up and sampled Sid Jones's coat from behind to see if it made tasty eating. But the high moment was Marcus's arrival. He leaped into Merryl's arms jabbering and rolling his eyes, scratching and smacking his lips. He reached out one hand graciously for the sergeant to kiss.

"Well, I'm blowed," said Sergeant Sid Jones.

CHAPTER 6

UNEXPECTED FUNDS

"HURRAH!" Milly yelled excitedly as she raced across the sunlit grounds of Summerleyton House. "Two glorious pieces of news. Come on, gang. Gather round while ye olde towne crier does her stuff!"

"If it's as important as it's noisy," Ken observed as he fed Uff-guff's last haddock down his undulating throat, "it's sure going to be tremendous."

The day was hot. The weather lately had been extremely sultry, threatening thunder for some time. August was drawing to a glorious close and no one regretted its passing more than the gang.

On Merryl fell the full weight and responsibility of the zoo. It had been her idea, so she had been the main pusher. The others were inclined to take the whole business in a mood of carefree enjoyment of the present, but Merryl was looking ahead. What of the day when they would be turned out of Summerleyton? What of the winter food bills, already hard to meet even when they could get stuff out of the hedgerows for nothing? What of the time when they must return to school themselves? Poor Aunt Penny if she were left to race across from the cottage every morning, noon, and night to feed the zoo inmates!

So Merryl's was the soberest face out of the laughing throng that ran to crowd round Milly.

"Number one piece of news," Milly burst out. "My dad's had to go rushing off to Glasgow on business, so that means that we can stay here a bit longer. I said so to him, but he looked mighty serious about it and began again that if we hadn't found anywhere else by the end of September we should have to give up the zoo and sell all the beasts!"

A groan went up.

"Don't get too upset," the girl went on cheerfully. "It's only August. Anything may happen in that time." She caught Merryl's eye and both remembered John Naylor's offer and his mysterious remarks. "The second news is that here's a letter inviting the Flaxstead Private Zoo to the grounds of Flaxstead Hospital for the Carnival. Of course, it's for charity, but they'll give us a bang-up tea for amusing the children. Eh—what fun?"

"How did *you* hear that? You're not treasurer or president," Teddy growled.

"No, but Dad's on the Hospital Entertainment Committee and he told me. He gave the letter to me to save a stamp." She handed it over. At the same moment Dodie came from Bramble Cottage with the post, which consisted of another letter, a very fat one for Merryl. Merryl shrugged away her fears and determined to live and enjoy things from day to day as the others did, for she could not help herself by worrying.

"Hello, what's this?" she cried as the torn envelope fluttered to the ground. "It's from Cummin's Zoo, in Perth. Seems to be a private one like ours. Listen! 'Dear Zoo Members—etc.—hmm—closing down our zoo owing to going abroad—hm—hm—dividing the creatures among our various friends and others as enthusiastic. Sending you some. Saw your name in an article in the Flaxstead paper a friend sent. Please accept Victory and Empress as a token of our feelings for fellow enthusiasts. Will box them and place them on south-bound train to reach you probably 4.30 on Saturday next. Please meet and acknowledge. Yours—etc.—etc.' "

"Oh, boy!" screamed Ken. "More zoo beasts! Oh, *what* will they be? Let's all guess."

"I hope they're not hippos or something frightfully huge like that," Merryl said anxiously.

"Idiot," Teddy comforted her. "You couldn't box a hippo. So you needn't worry—they can't be too outsize. But 'Saturday next' is today, isn't it?"

"We'll all go up to meet the darlings," Dodie cried. "I feel that Victory and Empress are going to be ducks."

"Then we'll eat them," Merryl said dryly. But she cheered up under the stress of general excitement.

"Better have a taxi to get them back here," Ken suggested, and Rupert barked approvingly, for he adored taxis.

"Not if they're giraffes," Dodie giggled.

"If they were giraffes, they couldn't have come by ordinary train," Teddy clinched the argument.

Excitement mounted all through the morning, until by four in the afternoon, when they were on their way to the station, sides were taken and argument ran high.

"Anyway, it'll mean two more for the Hospital Carnival on Wednesday next," Milly said.

When they got to the station, two of the three taxis available were in, so Teddy booked them provisionally. A distant whistle announced the approach of the four-thirty.

"Here it comes," Dodie squeaked as the long train clanked in, bumping and jarring over the points into the station.

They all made a bee-line for the baggage wagon at the rear.

"Dogs?" Milly cried, her face going white as she thought of rivals to her beloved Rupert. A perfect storm of barking could be heard clear down the platform to the booking-office.

"Oh, so you've come for them animiles, 'ave you?" the guard said, grinning as Teddy presented the invoice. "We shall all be glad to be quit of them, I must say. Biggest responsibility I've 'ad for years! And *eat*—they'd eat anyone out of hearth and home! 'Ow are you taking them? They bust them flimsy crates they was in back at Tooting Norbury, and they 'ave been flip-flapping round the flipping van hever since."

"D'you mean they're loose?" Dodie screamed.

"Of course they're loose. 'Ere they comes!"

Two magnificent sea-lions stood in the opening of the van, their keen whiskered faces gazing out, their front flippers raising them up to the alert position. They turned their heads from side to side and barked sonorously.

The gang collapsed as one man under a weight of mixed feelings, and the guard eyed them in deep sympathy.

"I'll give you a hand up to the taxis," he offered.

"Victory and Empress!" Merryl cried to them when she could get a little of her breath back. Immediately the sea-lions, hearing their names, stopped barking and with the most extraordinary lunging 'hirple' on their flippers, which were almost as mobile as a four-footed creature's legs, they bustled out of the van and raced across the platform, scattering the shrieking passengers. They reached

Merryl, crowded up to her, and barked expectantly in her face.

"That's all right, darlings," she cried, fearlessly stroking the shiny black skulls while they wiggled their whiskers at her. "You're going to be ever so happy with us!"

"You go first," Teddy whispered hoarsely. "They've taken a fancy to you and maybe they'll follow."

"Come on, darlings," Merryl said and led the way. People herded nervously out of her path and one youngster burst out crying, its face smothered in its mother's skirts.

Bump, bump, went the sea-lions energetically. Shepherded by the breathless gang, the guard and two porters, they reached the taxis.

"Here, I say," the driver of the first remonstrated "This ain't playing the gime. You didn't say hanimals!"

"Oh, *please!*" Merryl beseeched imploringly, while Victory, unnoticed, sampled the porter's trousers and sniffed his distaste of the flavour. "Unless you help we shan't ever get to Summerleyton House on the roads."

The man was melted by her appealing face. "Okay, miss," he said gruffly. "One 'ad better go in heach."

Which was by no means an easy matter. Empress certainly allowed herself to be assisted in, and, after an attempt to climb on to the seat and continue on straight through the taxi window had been frustrated, Teddy and Dodie got in with her and slammed the door.

Not so Victory. He gave one disgusted sniff at the dark interior, barked in wildest defiance and with a light shuffle of his supple body evaded the hands bent on securing him and made off down the station, scattering appalled children and frenzied adults as he went.

Empress became extremely excited at this, and the others were too much occupied holding her to be able to help Merryl, Milly and Ken, who galloped after him yelling desperately to him to stop, for they were terrified lest he should get out into the open street and be killed. And then they saw what it was that the sea-lion's astute nose had told him about. A porter unloading fish-boxes from a goods-train on number two platform had let one box down rather too smartly. The rotten wood of that fish-box, which had made many a journey from Great Yarmouth in its time, burst open and a stream of silver sprats oozed out.

"*Wukk-ah wukk-ah!*" barked Victory, in a tumult of excitement at the smell, which was as exciting to him as roast beef would be to the scared porter. He reached the delicious mess and pointed eagerly with his nose, his large velvet eyes alive with mute appeal. The man, who seemed to think that he had better get on the right side of the sea-lion, tossed him a handful of crushed sprats, and Victory snapped them up in mid-air, the muscles rippling along his satin neck.

The crowd closed in in a respectful ring and cheered. Finally a bobby appeared.

"Oh dear!" Merryl sighed, for she seemed to have fallen foul of the law lately.

"Bit of an obstruction, what?" the officer began cheerfully, wetting a stub of pencil to make notes. His beat was very dull, and this situation offered a change. Then he caught sight of Victory. "Blooming performing seal," he grunted in a slightly less-assured voice. "You'll have to get it out of here. Who owns this seal?"

"Sea-lion," Ken corrected wickedly. "I wish you could help us into that taxi with him, officer. The force is always so full of ideas!"

Robert looked at him sharply, for his tones had blended skilfully many emotions. But the boy's face was inscrutable and the man could not help feeling faintly flattered. He had spent a misunderstood youth. But he scratched his head in doubt.

"Not being born with hands and feet like a human, he can't offer a paw to be led by," the policeman complained. "I hardly think it would do to pick him up, either."

But thankfully Victory, having finished the fish, heard the cries of his partner imprisoned in the taxi and began humping along to join her. They got him in and shut the door and the crowd melted regretfully away. Ken mopped his brow. The taxi seemed to be very full of sea-lion. The air reeked of stale fish, and Victory was anything but a peaceful travelling companion. He rested *on* and against their feet and he weighed heavily, for he was a fine specimen. Every other second he was heaving and digging at them with his flippers trying to raise himself to see out. It was a good thing that he bit no one. But evidently both beasts had been almost household pets and used to travelling and being handled. He was singularly sweet-tempered too, for when Ken accidentally trod on his hind flipper he did not bite but gave a startled and pained bark as if he could not have believed it of anyone.

It was when they were once more back at the zoo and had paid the two taximen a staggering sum— for they said they'd never get the smell of fish off the cushions—that Merryl looked at her new charges uneasily.

They stood before her on the grass, front flippers bent outwards, their heads on one side, whiskers trembling gently as they sniffed the country airs of dried grass and scorching garden-flowers. A bland look of expectancy sat on their amiable faces as if to say, what next?

"It's a pond they want," Merryl whispered,

worried. "That's what they must have and yet you can't expect Uff-guff to give his up, and it is too small, anyway. Only one could get in at a time and then he could not turn round."

It was Teddy who solved this problem. "I know!" he yelled and leaped up to harangue them, his eyes blazing. "Only it means *work*!"

"We haven't been afraid of that up to now," Milly muttered sulkily.

"There's the stream that runs through that plantation fifty yards away. It's tidal."

"What of it?" Dodie sneered. "That's not a pond."

"No, but look: we're going to be chased out of here so it doesn't matter a pin what we do, and anyway it can be drained again!"

"What are you raving about?" Ken cried. "I can't bear much more. I'm tired *now* and at the very thought of more work my inside turns right over. It's frightfully distressing, and not one of you blighters cares a giddy hoot."

"The sunk rose-garden! All the roses are dead, but it's largely paved. We'll divert the stream, fill it, and it'll be a pond two hundred yards long by forty wide, and *then* the overflow can go out at the lower end and rejoin the stream!"

"Oh, boy! What a notion," Dodie said, too awed by the magnificent breadth of the plan to do more than whisper.

"Picks and shovels," Merryl cried excitedly. "There are crowds in the old toolshed. Come on!"

"But the water——?" Milly quavered almost stupidly. "How can we? Directly we begin diverting the stream——"

"You don't do it that way, goose," Dodie said. "Even I saw that. You make the cut from the dry end and let the water in last!"

"And we let it in when the tide is up, so getting salt water, which sea-lions need," said Teddy.

That deed remained an epic in the history of Flaxstead Zoo. Here and now it can be said that so ornamental was the resultant lake that it was never drained again, and later the children swam in it and held a water carnival, playing games with those magnificent swimmers, Victory and Empress, which became a feature of the zoo. But that was long after.

Through two hot arid days they toiled. Their hands became raw and then hardened up. Their backs ached so that they could not straighten when the lunch-break came. Aunt Penny remonstrated, Mr. Carter pleaded. In the children's eyes was a fanatical light of endeavour and they toiled on. They got to the stage when they spoke no more to one another, but hacked and dug in silence. Did any dare break this rule with idle chatter they hurled clods at him so that he sank under abuse.

A channel two feet deep by two wide they cut

through the rich black soil of the garden. The perspiration tickled their faces and they wiped it off with grimy hands with the most remarkable results. And then at last, both channels were finished and all that remained was a wedge of earth between the stream water and the new cut.

"You know," Teddy said, rubbing his aching back, "when we cut that it'll be a trifle messy. Let's get into our swimming things."

So, much to the amusement of Marcus, they prepared for the final act. The ape was disgusted with life. First there had been that huge blowing lump of an elephant to spoil his little paradise. Uff-guff had not made much difference certainly, for he was a fool bird anyway. But these barking horrors the sea-lions—why the humans had gone completely nuts over them, much to the sorrow of a poor ape, for he felt that a fellow needed plenty of attention and he thought himself neglected. Diccon too seemed put out. When he heard the sea-lions barking from the toolshed, where they were being housed for the time being, he whirled up his trunk and trumpeted shrilly. A nasty jealous light wavered in his little eyes, but he shuffled at his pickets and said nothing.

The zoo had been officially closed lately, for it was impossible to do more than they were doing.

"Dig like fun—she's *going*—she's gone!" Teddy screamed to his gang, leaping about in the squelchy mess, his broad bare feet splashing up the roily ooze.

"Look out," Merryl cried and jumped for safety. Ken bounded for the bank, missed his footing and fell back flat just as the lips of soil curled out under the pressure from the stream and burst. The water washed along the new cut, rolling the luckless Ken over so that he rose spluttering and yelling for air, crying out that he was drowned.

"I must have artificial respiration," he demanded. "One of you lazy funks ought to be giving it me. If someone doesn't do something I shall expire here and now and they'll come on you for the funeral expenses."

"There won't be any," Teddy replied brutally. "We'll tie a stone to you and sink you in the new pond."

They stood watching the water rise. It was a thrilling sight and it was all their own work! The stream raced along the cut and spread swiftly over the floor of the rose-garden. Leaves, chips, stalks and straw, the muddy water bore them all along to swirl slowly round and round as the pond filled.

"Looks messy," Milly moaned. "I thought it would be all lovely and clear like a bath."

"So it will be when it's settled," Dodie comforted.

They could not tear themselves away. Inch by inch the water rose, till Ken, trying it, said that it was up to his knees already, and still it went on filling. When the water at last reached the outlet, the pond was a great mirror fully ten feet deep at the lowest place and with plenty of shallows and ledges for the sea-lions to play on.

Victory and Empress were unlocked and brought to the scene of the gang's triumph, and they set their seal of satisfaction on it by immediately diving into the pond, supple as smooth furry eels, to chase each other round and round, rushing up the banks, leaping and gambolling like water-kittens.

"D'you know," Merryl observed next day, when, stiff from their toil, they took an easy day, "Marcus and Diccon *don't approve?*"

"What's Uff-guff said about it?" Ken demanded anxiously.

"Non-party, as far as I can tell, but then that greedy bird doesn't care a hoot as long as he's fed."

"He isn't greedy," his champion said very hotly; "not as greedy as a certain person who had three ice-cream tubs this morning."

"Two; I dropped one," Merryl corrected serenely. "No, but it's true. You watch."

They could see Marcus playing sulkily with a solid rubber ball Aunt Penny had given him, but his heart was not in the game. Every little while he stopped, flapped his hands and jabbered his lips, then put out his tongue, slowly, slyly, as a child does who knows that it is rude but who wants to annoy someone. He glanced sideways at Diccon as if to see whether the big beast were impressed with the ape's daring defiance of the humans. The elephant eyed him more tolerantly, gently twisting up his trunk to lay it in a coiled ring against his forehead and blowing a little.

Marcus hitched a little closer, chattering conversationally. He sat down to scratch exhaustively, one long arm over his shoulder, his lips moving in sympathetic motion to his efforts.

"*Chee, chee, chee!*" Marcus pointed out and suddenly stopped scratching to trundle his ball to the elephant's feet. Diccon moved carefully, for like all elephants he had a horror of stepping on little soft things, but he did not look ill-pleased at what was evidently an attempt to win his interest.

"They're just like a couple of babies, spoiled things!" Milly giggled.

Marcus rose on his hind legs and ambled up to Diccon, knuckling the ground as he moved. Teddy frowned.

"Diccon'll kill him," he said, startled. "The chimp's never allowed himself to get so near since the affair of the stolen hay."

"Sit tight, idiot!" Merryl cried, pulling him back. "This is bringing them together."

Diccon's trunk had reached out, but he made no attempt to knock the ape down or brain him. Marcus placed his wrinkled black hand on the curling trunk and next moment he was swung aloft to the post of honour, where he sat looking for insects, which he destroyed by eating them. He kept up a running commentary to his new pal as he worked.

"I'm staggered!" Dodie said helplessly. "They both felt so out of things actually that they agreed to hold a truce. And then some people say animals aren't fascinating."

Next day was the Hospital Carnival and there was a lot to do. The gang almost regretted their invitation, for the pond looked so blue and the day was so hot and sticky that a swim would have been ideal. Victory was lured out, but Empress refused the most seductive baits, so they decided she must stay behind. The Nubian goat got an extra grooming and had a bow tied round his neck, at which he simpered so deliciously that Ken could hardly brush him for laughing.

"That's an idea—dressing up," Teddy said. "Last year they gave prizes for the best costumes!"

"Does that mean that you're going with a rosette round your cauliflower ear as a prize poodle?" Dodie asked unkindly.

"If you will I'll give you a tanner," Ken offered in huge delight, and ducked to avoid the clod of earth thrown at him.

Teddy retired to the toolshed, where he could be heard working away, laughing wildly and hammering. Marcus they made a complete fool of, for they dressed him in a pair of flannel shorts and one of Teddy's shirts and fastened his long feet into a pair of old-fashioned button boots that had belonged to Aunt Penny's grandma. He was flattered at first and let them do it, but when he stood forth no one could stand for laughing.

The sight of his little bullet-domed head emerging from the clean shirt and his bowed legs spreading the natty shorts, to end in the elegant little button boots, made the gang roll upon the grass and choke and foam.

Marcus grew angry and danced, and one boot flew off, but they were too weak to retrieve it and anyway it was nearly time to set out for the Hospital, for Lady Morden was coming to open the Carnival at three.

"How is Victory going?" Merryl asked anxiously.

"What about the wheelbarrow?" Milly faltered.

"Yes, and I'm to push it, I suppose?" Ken said, thrusting his face close to hers and grimacing horribly.

"Oh, don't," she whimpered. "There—we won't take him if you'd rather. You scare me!"

"We will, then. I've had an idea, only I must pop over to Miss Penny's to borrow something!"

"You can't; you haven't time," Dodie screamed, but he had gone.

When he returned he had shed all his clothes except shorts and belt. Over them he had draped an old fox-fur tie borrowed from the good aunt, and he bore her muff upon his head as a fur hat. The rest of him was just rich brown sunburn.

"I'm going as Robinson Crusoe," he yelled, "with Victory as my Man Friday!"

Teddy bounded out of the toolshed carrying a shiny black top hat of enormous proportions which he had been making in plywood and had brushed over with some liquid lampblack. There was a rope attached to tie it on with. Diccon in his top hat looked absolutely priceless! He sensed that they thought he was unusually smart, for he wig-wagged his ears and said: *Phrumph*. Marcus was put on his back, sulking in his shirt and shorts, which, if they had not been of the stoutest materials, would long ago have been in shreds.

The Flaxstead Hospital was this side of the town, but it was quite a long way and Ken, perspiring behind his wheelbarrow, in which the astonished sea-lion coughed and barked, felt as if it were ten miles.

When they got there they found the grounds very pretty. Paper garlands and paper lanterns were strung from the trees, an old marquee had been turned into a tea-tent, and there were games and sideshows and a fortune-teller.

But the arrival of the Flaxstead Private Zoo was the great moment of the day, which was never forgotten. First into the field marched Diccon and wizened face and wistful eyes peering round her skirts. Growing more and more bewildered at the laughs and stares which his burst shorts evoked, and being unable to rid himself of the garment, he had wandered up on to the platform to get away.

Lady Morden cleared her throat magnificently and smiled, though the effort was a trifle strained.

"With no ulterior motive," she resumed, "with nothing hidden from you——"

Marcus bobbed out of sight, to reappear on the other side, and the crowd became hysterical.

"Is there anything peculiar in what I am saying?" she asked in tones which could have been used to keep the ices freezing in the marquee.

"Bravo!" one man shouted.

Marcus peered up at the woman's face, the fingers of one hand at his lips while with the other he held together the rent in his rear.

"I declare the Carnival open!" Lady Morden cried, vanquished and genuinely frightened, for she thought that the heat had affected the crowd and she felt quite faint. As she swung round to leave the platform she saw the ape, who immediately began to flutter his hands at her and chatter as if imploring pity.

"Oh!" she cried. "So those wretched children brought you did they? Well, all I can say is you are better behaved than these people!" And she left and drove home at once and had hysterics, while the

"That's all right," Mr. Smith said, looking at her curiously. "I'm in no hurry. I don't start back till tomorrow; I've got business in Flaxstead. Then I'll come round and pick up the ape."

He left them and a deep gloom settled on everyone. Somehow, no one had ever *expected* to lose Marcus even though they had talked of it. How miserably quiet the place would be when his cheeky chatter was heard no more! Even Diccon seemed to sense that something was wrong, for he trumpeted and squealed till they thought he was hungry and rushed forward more food for him, but he kicked it aside with one foot and went on complaining.

No one could get any comfort, now, going to look at the wonderful new pond, where Victory and Empress were rolling and surface-diving, quite careless of the gloom which fate had cast over the zoo. Marcus became extremely nervous again, whimpering and glaring.

"What *is* it, Marcus darling?" Merryl asked, feeling like a mother. "Oh dear, I wish you could talk!"

She wondered if he were getting enough exercise.

"Come on; we'll go to Bramble Cottage to get the post," she suggested and took hold of his hand. Usually Marcus adored going for walks and behaved with the same exuberance as a dog shows, but now he hung back, crying dolefully, pulling at her dress, his face twitching, his very ears appearing to stand out from his head with fright. When she tried force he gave a scream and tore himself out of her grasp to bolt away and hide in the toolshed. She had to shrug and start off alone.

A thick coppice lay on her left, the relic of a vast ornamental shrubbery now grown wildly out of control and thick as a jungle with exotic trees and shrubs from many lands. For this reason it had always fascinated Merryl, but she had never had time to explore its densities.

Now, to her amazement, she heard a sound within its depths, an indescribable sound rather like an engine running but not so smoothly. There was a rasping quality about the noise.

"Gracious, it's some trick of the boys," she thought, for anyone living long with Ken and Teddy had to be hardened against surprises of all kinds. She parted the wand-like stalks of a semi-tropic plant and peered into the gloom, then began to force her way in, crashing her path into the stuffy space smelling of old leaves and damp moss.

At the first sound she made, the engine stopped and an alert, listening silence fell on the warm air. There was something very queer in all this, and Merryl caught herself wondering if it would be best to go for one of the boys or even John Naylor. There might be something hidden here which he wanted. In that case, she'd better investigate first.

Panting for breath, for it was very close in the

shrubbery, she pushed on, but she could hear nothing more, for she was making too much noise herself. But she tried to keep on in the general line of where the noise had been. She paused to stare ahead, and her heart stood still.

A pair of huge eyes were watching her in perfect golden calm! It was too shadowy to make out to what they belonged, but they were live, for she could almost see the expression floating in their limpid depths. They disappeared suddenly as they closed, and the warm dark void without them was worse. Merryl's heart was hammering so that she could feel it in her throat and it made her feel sick. It was a pretty horrid sensation and a pretty horrid situation and she knew that she was scared stiff.

What on earth was *there*? The eyes were so big and luminous, far too big for a prowling tom-cat's or even a lost dog's, though now she came to think of it there was a peculiar, almost doggy, smell hanging about the bushes. Suddenly the eyes were watching her again. She forced herself to break this spell of fear. On knees trembling in spite of her resolution she pushed forward and stood looking into a tiny clearing. Even then, face to face with reality, she could not believe that it was not a dream. Things like this just didn't happen in quiet, peaceful England.

A big lion was lying there staring at her! He had been dressing his fur and grunting and puffing as he did so and that was the extraordinary sound she had heard. Now he was not purring. In terrified fascination she could make out the noble, sulky-looking face, the unwinking eyes, the coarse neck-fur tipped with darker hairs, the easy muscles moving under the tan beige hide.

Suddenly the lion closed his eyes again, and the first wave of comfort came to the girl. Of course— she had read of that—the big cats could not stand an unwinking human stare. Sheer fright had kept her eyes glued to the lion's face. But how had the beast come there and from where? Had he smelled the reassuring animal smell of the zoo and fancied that among others of his kind he might find sanc-tuary? Clearly he was escaped from somewhere. And yet there was no other zoo for hundreds of miles. Reason began to whisper to the girl that she had better do something about the situation.

"Hello," she said, feeling awful. But at first sound of her voice the beast stirred and rose on short powerful legs, its long, rather rangy body looking thin and fallen in. It drooped its big head as if tired and yawned slowly, despairingly.

"I believe," Merryl thought with a flash of insight, "that he's as hungry as he can be."

The big beast shuffled forward, and it was then that it took all the girl's nerve and grit to stand her ground. She guessed from his manner that the lion was fairly tame, but she also knew that if she were to turn and run all his hunting instincts would make him follow and strike her down. And her retreat was not open. So she waited and wondered if this was how people felt in the Roman arena ages ago.

The lion's hot breath was on her hands, his heavily whiskered face was only a foot away, and then suddenly she was not afraid any more. An expression of mute appeal and misery was in those yellow eyes that turned away blinking from her stare.

"Oh, you *poor* thing!" she said, a warm rush of sympathy making her voice shake where fear had not. Without thinking, she put out her hand and laid it on the tawny head and had time to think absently how wiry the beast's coat felt. He pushed his head against her knees in a caressing gesture and a low rumbling grew in his throat, a throbbing purr as pathetic as a stray cat's.

"Well, if you'll come along out of this," Merryl suggested, trying to pull at his mane to give him the idea, "I think I could find something for you to eat. There's half a pork-pie from our lunch."

But the lion absolutely refused to budge. He had no doubt escaped, not from any deep-seated cunning but simply because his cage door had been left accidentally open. Cage-bred of cage-bred parents, he was quiet and sweet-tempered and, as a consequence, terrified of his liberty. To him the clang of his cage door meant peace, security and good meals, and now he had none of those things

to his paw. He was famished and could find not
so much as a rat to eat. He longed for human company, but was so scared that he could not bring
himself to come out from the little heaven he had
found for himself. The rush and turmoil on the
roads had so terrified him that he had slunk along
in hedge bottoms, knocking off an occasional rabbit
for his supper.

Merryl considered him a moment, her eyes soft
with pity, for he was gazing at her in earnest
hungry hope, expecting her to know by instinct his
wants, as they had always known them where he
came from.

"There's no help for it, Leo," she said firmly. "I
shall have to get help to make you come out of this.
Don't get worried. I'll be back!"

As she crashed her return way through the bushes
she wondered if the uncannily keen senses of the
ape and elephant had told them of the lurking lion
and been the cause of Marcus's flat spin. She burst
out of cover a dreadful sight, for the heat and the
dust of the bushes had streaked her face, hands and
frock with black lines. Her curly hair had been
wrenched from its bobby-pins and lay in a tangled
matted mass. But her eyes were snapping, her cheeks
ablaze.

"Ken, Teddy, help!" she called. "Can you spare
a minute and we'll want a rope and that half
pork-pie!"

The boys stared at her as she rushed into camp, and Dodie's mouth dropped open. Milly had gone home for the afternoon.

"*Darling*," Dodie began, "I thought you'd gone for the letters. Did you tumble or something?"

"No, of course not," Merryl answered almost airily. "I've got a lion, but I can't move him and I thought if we all——" She saw consternation light up their faces. "What's wrong? What are you all goggling at?"

"You're feeling quite all right?" Dodie questioned anxiously. "I mean—that carry-off the other day; it might make anyone feel queer."

"Don't be so soppy," Merryl snapped. "I'm as right as rain, only this lion——"

"What lion?" Dodie asked hollowly, while the two boys exchanged meaning glances which infuriated the girl—just as if she were 'bats', she thought resentfully.

"The lion I am telling you about. I've got it in the shrubbery!"

"Look," Teddy said kindly, "how about going and lying down a bit, you know?"

"Oh, you make me wild!" Merryl stormed. "If you don't want to help or are scared, you needn't. I'll get poor Leo out somehow by myself, but I'll have that bit of good rope and that half pie." Raging at their silly frightened faces, she got the things for herself and then set off back, taking no further notice of them. Their certainty obviously shaken, they followed her, bewildered.

"Did you say a—a *lion*?" Dodie gasped at last as they reached the shrubbery.

"You heard," Merryl replied rather rudely, but she was busy planning how to persuade Leo to come out. She parted the bushes and dived in. The branches continued to rustle, so she knew that Dodie, Ken and Teddy were following, and a grim little smile played round her mouth.

"Leo, Leo!" she called softly, and a welcoming roar shook the place. Merryl was prepared, the others were not. There is something awful about the roar of a lion, even a tame one. Some quality in its deep coughing vibrations shakes one's very heartstrings, dries the inside of the mouth, and makes the knees flap together.

Teddy gave one strangled gasp and would have fled if by himself, but his manhood would not let him quail before a girl. Ken went as white as a sheet of paper and his eyes bulged until, as Dodie said afterwards, he reminded her of an indignant rabbit. Dodie sat down where she was, for her knees gave way completely. But Merryl pushed on.

"Okay, I'm coming, Leo dear!"

"Suffering snakes!" Teddy whispered to the other two. "We don't know our Merry apparently. Here's where I believe anything she says in future. What a sticky place to be caught in if—if it charges!"

"What are you doing, Merry?" Dodie asked humbly, pushing up behind her chum as soon as she could move again. She peered with popping eyes into the gloom, where she could just make out the shape of the lion. But Merryl had forgotten her annoyance.

"I've got the pie for him," she explained, "then I'll tie this round his neck, and if we all pull it'll give him the idea of following, but if he resists of course there's nothing we can do; we shall have to go for help."

She fed Leo, who took the pie very readily and seemed to look for more. A patient, disappointed sigh escaped him. Moving slowly, for she remembered an animal article which warned one of hurried acts with wild things, for nothing scares them so quickly, Merryl made a running bowline and got it round the beast's neck. She pulled gently.

"Come on, big stupid," she urged softly. "Catch hold and help pull, you three!"

They pulled, digging their heels in to get a purchase, and Leo resisted, partly because he was afraid to come out, partly because he was warm, dry and comfy and was a conservative beast, anyway.

"Might as well try to move Bramble Cottage," Ken grunted and then sat down hard and suddenly on a partly uncovered root, as did the others, for Leo suddenly changed his mind and came bounding softly from hiding, hurtling the canes and bushes apart and yet moving with far less noise than the slimmer children.

He leaped over them as they sprawled on the path, and looking up they had one second's uncanny sight of Leo's underside as he passed above them. Then the pull came on the line which they had wrapped round wrists and arms so that they straightened up off the ground like galvanised nine-pins and flew after Leo. He bounded out into the open, dragging the four children along, and they bounded too, desperately trying to keep their feet. Seen from the wings, it was quite an impressive sight. It was quite a pity on the whole that Milly had gone home.

Leo continued on and Marcus saw him coming. If a black-haired ape could go pale then he did. They saw just one streak of him and he was gone in the direction of Summerleyton House. But Leo was not interested in him. All he wanted to do was to find more to eat, and with unerring instinct he made for the lean-to where they kept the food-basket and then only did he stop, with his head in a hamper, his flanks heaving as he ate, his tufted tail moving in slow appreciation from side to side.

"What was in it?" Ken mouthed the question.

"Ham sandwiches," Dodie replied with forced calm, "and the rest of that cold chicken from the farm. *That's* it, going now!" as loud sounds of cracking bones came from the hamper.

They were naturally a trifle nervous, all of them, as to Leo's next move, for there was no blinking the fact that he was the first really dangerous animal they had handled. Suppose he attacked and polished off Uff-guff or tried to savage the sea-lions? *He* would see no harm in it, but it would be pretty awful. So when he pulled his head out and stood regarding them with benign pleasure while a huge tongue, broad and flat and moist, was taking the sandwich crumbs off his whiskers, they were much relieved to see that he no longer looked quite so hungry.

"Where's he going to sleep?" Ken asked. "It's me and Teddy on tonight."

"Toolshed?" Merryl suggested, for that was their only good lock-up.

So the toolshed it was, but Leo took a dim view of it and neither boy slept very well, as Leo's baffled roars were nerve-tickling even when you knew he would not break out.

It is only natural, however, to want to play off on others tricks with which fate has 'had' you. Ken and Teddy had only one idea next morning and that was to make Milly sneer as they had sneered and then confront her with the presence of Leo. One thing spoiled everyone's pleasure and that was that Marcus had not come back. They all loved the black rascal, but besides being sorry for his terror there was the unhappy fact that Mr. Smith had said he would call for the ape today and if they could not produce him might think they were holding out on him.

Merryl said straight out that it was a mean trick to try and have fun at Milly's expense, and she and Dodie would not help. But Ken and Teddy, now completely over their fear of the lion, brought him out, fed him into an extra good temper and then tied him up in the corner of the shelter where Milly always slept when on duty and where she kept her little box with mirror, comb and other trifles, for she was fussy that way.

"We'll tell her we've found her a lion," Teddy smirked, "and say it's on her bed and she'll scoff or else think it's a stuffed toy we mean, and then she'll go into the darkish corner——"

"Yes," Merryl said seriously, "and what will you think if she has hysterics?"

"Pooh!" Ken said, but he looked uneasy.

Milly came tripping and singing along about nine-thirty. She was very conscientious about taking her turns and had never been late yet. She came skipping up to the camp.

"Hello, gang!" she cried cheerfully, and any-one not as full of their own ideas would have seen that she was bursting with some story or titbit of zoo gossip.

"Oh, I say, Milly," Teddy asked carelessly, "d'you like lions? There's one on your bed!"

The boys waited hopefully for the incredulous scream or the loud disbelief. Milly merely looked pleased.

"Oh, goody, you've got him! I wondered if he might wander here." She looked with amazement at their crestfallen faces, and the girls' merrily laughing ones.

"Watcher mean—we've got him?" Teddy growled.

"Oh, it's all over Flaxstead. He's escaped from a travelling circus and the police are combing the village. And, by the way, it's *your* circus, Merryl, Joe Black's Circus. And he said he'd come and look you up when he was in this district and he's coming. Perhaps the lion heard him talking and got in first—ha, ha, ha!" Milly finished. "May I see him?"

"Yes, dear, you shall," Merryl cried, and she and Dodie took the delighted girl to Leo. They had never liked poor, silly, scared Milly so *awfully* much as they did now. The boys slunk away to do the morning's grooming and later Teddy went to phone Joe Black and invite him to pick up his lion and let the police know.

At eleven-thirty, Mr. Smith came again and with him a familiar figure whom Teddy and Merryl greeted with joy. Joe Black was jolly as ever and his white hair curled even more wildly than before.

He greeted them with loud cries and hearty back slaps and asked after Diccon. But who was to tell Mr. Smith? Merryl was pushed forward. It was a startling admission of her moral courage that she always was pushed forward to the sticky jobs. So she told him as quickly as she could, and her voice was unsteady with woe about it.

"We're awfully sorry. He was scared of Leo and bolted. I've searched everywhere, but I'll have another try because, of course, we feel dreadful about it."

Joe Black looked on twinkling, and Mr. Smith laughed kindly.

"This is rather a joke," he said. "You see, all last night I was thinking of you all here and doing so well with this place and Moko so happy with you and I had decided that it would be criminal to take him back!"

"You mean you're giving him to us," Merryl almost screamed.

"Well, it looks like that, I must say."

"*How lovely!*" she whispered, and though her words were commonplace the way she said them made all the difference to the man. The gang closed round him and hugged and yelled.

"If that's all settled," Joe Black exclaimed, with dry humour, "what about giving me a say in? I want you all to come over tonight for the show after you've put the animals to bed. Now don't begin

saying that someone must stay with them! I'll
have two men drive the box-car over for my lion
and one can stay here on guard for you. And I
must thank you for looking after my beast. I bet
there's a story there, for though he's as tame as an
old tabby I bet it took some guts to tackle him on his
face-value. But as Salani said when he met you up
north: 'She have the touch with the little brothers
of men; she will never be afraid.'" He nodded at
Merryl, who got hot all over and wished he hadn't
singled her out, but the others cheered generously.

"Now, I mean all of you, your aunts and uncles,
and anyone who'll come, and you too, Mr. Smith,
if you'll humour an old circus man. Show starts
at eight, and I've a surprise for you, children!"

But he would not say what it was and took himself off chuckling secretively after inspecting and
admiring the zoo. The afternoon was one of growing excitement. Milly had not seen a circus for
ages and Dodie never *had* seen one. The work went
like play and the only shade on their spirits was the
fact that Marcus was still missing. Then, suddenly,
after tea, when the lion had been fetched away, he
appeared, famished and cold—ice cold.

"Oh where's he been hiding?" Merryl asked
anxiously, cuddling the shivering scrap of ape-dom
to her, while Dodie chafed the frozen wrinkled
feet. "Funny-coloured sand he has, too, all over
him!"

"Well, anyway, he's home," Ken observed, "so there's nothing to spoil our enjoyment."

Even Aunt Penny declared it was rather a lark to see a circus again. She had changed quite a lot these last weeks and seemed younger and gayer, but then, as Merryl reflected, counting it up one day, she could not be much over forty and for Aunt Penny that probably felt still quite young. John Naylor was having tea with her when Teddy took over the invitation, but he could not make one of the party, he said regretfully, as he had a busy evening in front of him in Flaxstead. Poor Miss Penny looked quite crestfallen.

The circus big top had been put up in a field just outside the town, and when they neared it in the velvet summer evening it looked fairylike with strings of coloured lights, the beams from big search-lights trained on the great painted entrance and the fancy costumes of the professionals; for, being a family affair, all helped to get the audience comfortably seated before entertaining them.

A pretty sprite in rose-coloured frills was selling tickets; their old friend the lion-tamer, in leopard skin and doeskin sandals, was showing people to their seats, and the clowns were everywhere being unusually useful, as if they had temporarily laid aside that habit of joyous fooling which is their right.

Word had been left at the box-office, and the

zoo party were all passed in and into the best seats
at five and sixpence each. Of the circus itself there
is no need to say anything. It was an excellent
show, much better than the average touring circus
twice its size. It was rather fun too in being friends
of the owners, as a dead set was made at the gang.
The clowns pointed them out and tried to get Ken
and Teddy to come and help them with their act,
but the boys were far too wily and laughingly
refused. The painted canvas horse with two men
inside, which can be rather alarming when it gets
loose and climbs out of the ring, came and sat
beside them and even offered Aunt Penny an arm.
The crowd enjoyed all this hugely, and it was a
good thing that the gang was not given to shyness.

But after it was all over, after the performing
lions and elephants and the trapeze artistes had
done their stuff and Dodie had made the decision
to run away and join a circus when she was older,
Joe Black took them behind the tents to see all his
pets.

Little Salani came up, shyly pleased to see Merryl
and Teddy again and eager to get to know the rest
of the gang. Aunt Penny invited everyone in sight
to tea at the zoo and everyone accepted with
jubilation.

"Now, this is my surprise," Joe Black said,
pausing before a big cage with one small wistful
inmate. "This is Norah, and her mother refuses

to feed her. We are bringing her up on a bottle, but we haven't the time—travelling—to give her all the care she needs. So I thought that——"

Merryl had gone quite pale with excitement. "D'you mean you'd leave her with us to bring up?" she asked breathlessly, eyeing the small lion-cub with its tawny spotted coat and melancholy air. All lion-cubs have serious, old-fashioned expressions as if shocked at their first sight of the world, and Norah was no exception. Her huge amber eyes held such a look of hopeless appeal that Milly expected any minute to see them brim over with tears.

"That's about the idea! I remember how you told me you'd love to have a lion, but I had my doubts till I saw how well you'd managed old Prince!"

"Oh, boy!" cried all the gang, and only Dodie whispered: "Will Marcus be scared again?"

"Not at a cub! He just couldn't be," Merryl answered. "He'll get to love it. It's different starting young to being met by a full-grown beast."

She turned out to be right in the long run, though Marcus took longer to 'come round' than she expected.

And so that is how a lion-cub came to be included in their zoo beasts.

"How are you going to get it home?" Aunt Penny asked, but the cry: "Carry her, of course, the fubsy darling!" settled that.

And carry her they did all that long moonlit walk
back, sharing the hot, heavy little burden jealously
and squealing with delight when Norah buried an
exploring nose in their necks. Her big soft feet
hung down peacefully, and it was hard to imagine
a time when no one, unless they knew her, would
dare go within reach of the big broad paws.

Merryl was disappointed with Marcus, for, confronted by the cub next day, he said *Chee, chee!*
in deep explosive disgust, putting one hand over
his eyes as if to shut out the horrible sight. He
continued to growl and grunt, thinking to attract
notice to himself, but when Dodie, in a wide apron,
sat down on a low stool, took the fat fubsy cub on her
knee and reached for the feeding bottle Ken had
warmed and prepared, the ape lost his head
completely.

Not only did he hurl his own delicious breakfast
of bananas and grapes into Uff-guff's pond, much
to the alarm of that gentle bird, but he literally
pranced with rage and bolted off among the trees
in the same direction as he had gone before. Merryl,
with lively memories of having to clean him up
before, went after him at once. But the rascal had
completely disappeared, though the girl hunted
through a wilderness of wild growth nearer the
house, where the park had been utterly neglected
and burdock and cow-parsley were waist-high
jungle.

All at once she came to a familiar opening in the ground, the drainpipe through which she had crawled so long ago, and there in the soft mud near its mouth was Marcus's footprints. So that was where the little wretch had been hidden, just out of sight but feeling himself safe!

"I'll soon have him out," Merryl thought and dived in.

Almost at once she knew that this was not the drainpipe. No, of course, it could not be—*that* was nearer the other wall round Summerleyton grounds.

"Must be an old fox's earth," she thought, "perhaps widened by the rain washing down it that stormy day. Marcus, Marcus!"

What a lot of extra work the dear little wretch made! And then all at once there was a sound of rushing and crumbling all about her as the rotten earth walls and flooring gave beneath her weight where the lighter chimp had passed without disaster. She said afterwards that only once before in her life had she felt quite such an awful feeling of terrified helplessness, and that was when learning to swim she stepped out of her depth.

But now she did not know what had happened. All she knew was that she was falling down into nothing, with the collapsing soil about her. She landed with a shock which so dazed her that she lay for a few moments with her eyes shut, trying to pretend to herself that it was a dream and hadn't really happened. The frightful idea that she had fallen downwards into the darkness was enough to make anyone afraid.

"Don't panic!" she told herself sternly, a familiar piece of advice with Merryl. Slowly she opened her eyes. She felt shaken and bruised, but there was no pain anywhere, so she hadn't broken anything!

In the darkness above her a blue moon glowed dimly and terror choked her till reason helped her out.

"Of course, you goose, that's the light filtering down what's left of the tunnel. Looks as if, like Alice in Wonderland, you've fallen a considerable distance, my child."

Cautiously she got up, her eyes growing more used to the gloom. She could see that the entrance was some twenty feet over her head and completely out of reach of anyone without wings.

"This is a jam to be in," she reflected, with all the calm of despair, and then nearly screamed as something came bounding and scuttering through the dark.

"*Chee, chee!*" yelled Marcus and flung himself upon her, overjoyed no doubt that a human should share this delicious hideout he had found so cleverly for himself.

"Oh, how you scared me," the girl cried putting her arms protectingly round the ape, for she knew that he was doomed as much as she. Probably before the miniature landslide it had been possible for the chimp to get in and out, but now he was cut off. Tears came into her eyes, and she was not to be blamed for them, because it was extremely unlikely that she would ever be found.

Who would think of poking down holes in the ground? Her screams would never reach the happy outer world. It was a sober thought that she must sit here slowly weakening in this underground gloom, all by herself.

"Oh, no, no!" she moaned, "I daren't; I'm frightened!"

Then a better mood came to her, for Merryl was essentially a fighter and seldom gave way to black despair for long. She remembered one or two things that were comforting. One was that in her skirt-pocket was an electric torch. She always carried one when it was her turn to do night-duty at the zoo. At any rate, she could look at this queer underground world into which she had fallen. The other was that she had a tin of barley-sugar on her and that must be iron rations until she was rescued.

She used the word rescued deliberately to herself.

"We'll each have a piece now to keep up our spirits," she told Marcus, and got out the tin. He pressed against her in hairy friendliness, quite of one mind with her about enjoying a sweet. She sucked hers thoughtfully while fumbling for the torch.

"My stars!" she cried, as her light flashed on, revealing her 'prison'. She had read of these caves in other parts of the world; surely there was one in France discovered only recently? They were the ancient relics of men who dwelled on earth countless ages ago and left their pictures on the walls. A rush of warm kinship—a strange feeling—for those forgotten races came to her with the drawings of the animals. Here was another zoo from the very dawn of the world, mighty mammoth and deer and dogs, running, leaping or feeding, drawn with that faithful picturesque detail and anatomical accuracy for which cave-paintings are so famous.

She knew that this discovery was tremendously important, for though there were such caves already in England, yet these drawings were so perfectly preserved.

"Oh, Marcus, what a find!" she whispered, and began exploring. From cave to cave she went, marvelling that a mere slide of earth had disclosed this world to her, and yet—was she the first who had been here?

She stopped amazed, for she had just entered a new cave much lower than the others, the rocky walls unadorned, the floor smoothed and levelled at a later date. Marcus chattered nervously now and pressed against her, fingering her skirt with his black fingers to give himself moral support by her nearness.

G

"Marcus," Merryl said solemnly, "I believe you have settled John Naylor's problem! This is where they stored the treasure of Summerleyton House!"

How well she could imagine the scene: lanterns swinging and smoking as serving men and maids came carrying books, papers, pictures and plate down out of the old house to hide them from Cromwell's men. Why had they never been returned to their places? Had those who hid them all fallen victim to the driving force of civil war, so that the secret died with them?

With trembling hands she pulled forward the monster picture-frames stacked against the walls, their pictures hidden. The dry atmosphere had preserved everything wonderfully; hardly anywhere was any mould. One glance at those paintings showed her art-treasures of great worth, and among them a family tree which went back to the Conquest. Among those names and in those papers Naylor would find the proof he sought.

She shook with great excitement and a cold sweat broke out on her skin as she thought of all that meant. He had promised that if he came to own Summerleyton the zoo should never have to move away.

They were safe—they need never move away! Then came another thought. There must be a connection with the cellars of the old house, and that was what that mysterious paper had meant. She hugged the astonished ape so hard that he squeaked and chittered his teeth at her.

Then in her joy she sat down and cried to think that her zoo was safe, where she had not shed a tear over her own troubles. At this the ape looked so appalled that she must laugh and dry her eyes. He blew his nose on his fingers to relieve his feelings, a disgusting habit taught him by those wicked boys.

A little groping revealed the door to the cellars, and with John Naylor's key she let herself through and two minutes later was in the sunshine of mid-morning and running across the lawns in freedom.

CHAPTER 8

SUMMER'S END

MERRYL never forgot the thrill of announcing her great discovery and being thanked by John Naylor in tones which showed how little hope he had really had of ever attaining his life's dream.

The next two weeks were so full of comings and goings, visits of archaeologists and experts, and consultations with solicitors, great men from big cities, that the zoo life was almost disorganised. But as Naylor's claim was sorted out and established, and cables sent singing under the seas to far-off lands where the present owner lived, it was finally made clear that Summerleyton House and grounds belonged to Naylor.

Things went back to normal and all rejoiced that Flaxstead Zoo was established now for all time, come rain or storm, good luck or ill!

Merryl began training Norah. "You can't expect her to grow into a perfect lady if we spoil her when she's young," she said firmly. "She's going to jolly well have her meals at the proper times and no snacks between however much she snarls for them!"

"How hard-hearted," Dodie exclaimed, shocked, but Merryl was right, and Norah responded from the first. Her beautiful eyes, with that look of melancholy surmise in their golden depths, followed the girl everywhere; she soon learnt the trick of standing up on her fubsy hind feet and hammering with her immense paws on anything near, a wall or door, to show her joy when the girl went to her.

"I'm sorry Marcus takes no notice of her," Milly said. "It's as if he were sulking again. He's frightfully pally and mushy with Diccon!"

"Pure jealousy," Merryl laughed. "Every new creature as it has come along he's taken a dislike to. But he can't quite make Norah out and he's the weeist bit afraid of her and so he keeps away."

"And *I* think you're all wrong!" Ken observed shrewdly. "Norah is the first *baby* animal we've had and Marcus would give his head to help look after her, but after the stand he's taken he doesn't know how to break it and make the first move. Quite human!"

"Well, that's an awful reflection on humans," Merryl said seriously. "Is that milk warm enough yet, Ken?"

"Yes," Ken cried, coming out of the 'cooking' corner with Norah's bottle.

Teddy appeared at this moment, pale and quivering with excitement. He had just been home for the letters and apparently he had found news of importance. "Come on, gang," he yelled, and they dropped everything and ran out to meet him.

"Anything wrong?" Dodie screamed in a panic, for she had not been back to the farm for twenty-four hours and imagined all sorts of horrors.

"No, nothing, but I met Naylor and—and he's going to marry Miss Penny—yes, truly—and they're going to live here and she's going to help with the creatures when we've got to go to school again. So there goes our last headache!"

They stood round stunned by this tremendous news.

"I am glad," Merryl said softly, "simply awfully glad!" And she was not thinking only of the zoo.

"You still look bursting with news! Anything more?" Milly asked.

The boy grinned. "I met Lady Morden shopping in Smith's and she appears to have forgotten all about her upset at the Carnival. She rushed across when she saw me, all smothery—you know —and told me excitedly that she thought our effort was *wonderful* and that she'd long ago done as she promised and cabled her relations abroad to send us exhibits!"

"*What?*" they all screamed.

"And she went on," Teddy said wickedly, "to say that they ought to be arriving *any time now!*"

"That's wonderful," Merryl said nervously. "I wonder how soon they'll begin coming in?"

"Yes," Teddy rambled on, "and I thought while the old fatty was in such a sunny mood I'd see if I could get any more help and so I said I *hoped* we'd be able to feed 'em. And she positively cooed at me and said that of course she'd *love* to help and that if the town had the advantage of a zoo it ought to help support it and she'd speak to all her friends, because of course they threw out *masses* of stuff at her home farm!"

"I daresay we can use it all," Ken muttered uneasily. "That reminds me, weren't we getting ready to feed Norah? Her milk will be getting cold."

Chattering, they wandered back into the lean-to, and lo! the milk-bottle had completely disappeared.

"You did put it down here?" Merryl asked, bewildered, and then they all paused to listen to strange sounds coming from the baby lion's enclosure, little crooning sounds of encouragement. Spellbound, they watched.

Marcus was sitting on the ground beside an astounded Norah, who was sitting bolt upright like a dog. The ape's long, hairy, powerful arm was round the cub's shoulders and in his other hand he had her bottle. Seizing his opportunity when she whined, he sought to introduce the rubber teat between her jaws, but she turned her head away pettishly. Marcus's protective instinct was thoroughly roused, however, for instead of losing his own temper, as was usual when he was thwarted, he persevered, puckering up his big rounded lips into an 'oh' of encouragement, holding the cub firmly and trying patiently to get her to take her breakfast. His feet, stretched out in front of him, opened and closed in sympathetic endeavour, the thumb-like big toe moving spasmodically.

"Chee, chee!" Marcus enthused, but Norah shuffled her big soft feet, and, turning her large soft eyes on the ape, said 'Won't' as plainly as print. 'Don't want it!'

"That's where you're wrong, sister!" Marcus seemed to be chatting amiably, and tried the bottle again. Norah gave a weary sigh, and the chimp, with commendable smartness, took the opportunity of her mouth being open to get in a quick hook to the jaw with his bottle. The rest was easy. Norah, comforted by the familiar warmth and taste, began to suck greedily, and Marcus, hardly able to contain his joy, chuckled and simmered and jabbered. His eyes, following the line of the descending level of milk, fairly popped with excitement, while his feet executed a heel dance to let off his emotions.

"The absolutely corking darling!" Merryl said, and Marcus turned and saw them all watching him. He enjoyed perhaps the greatest triumph he had ever known.

But they were late already with the work and had to tear themselves away from the fascinating sight. Uff-guff had still to have his breakfast, and Victory and Empress were barking lustily from their pond, imagining that their meal had been overlooked in the general excitement, which it nearly had been.

Milly, hearing a lorry or a car driving up to the gates and honk for attention, went at once to see what was wanted. Milly had changed much and become self-reliant and dependable; the gang could hardly believe there had been a time when they had been inclined to laugh at her. She returned now followed by two men carrying crates on their heads.

"Could you put them here, please?" she said with cool assurance, indicating the corner where they kept their stores. The men deposited the crates and then stared round with so much hopeful curiosity on their faces that she took them on a personally conducted tour of the zoo. They left in a cloud of admiring remarks.

"Who were those jossers?" Ken asked when Milly got back.

"From Lady Morden's head gardener, some lettuces that will bolt before she can get through them. She sent to say that Diccon, the goat and the hare might like them."

"How kind!" Merryl exclaimed. "My stars, if people are going to help feed them we're absolutely sitting pretty." She glanced round as Teddy came up. "Heavens, what's that you've got?"

"Just left at the gate. Five pounds of slightly over-ripe tomatoes from Smithers in the High

Street," Teddy grinned. "I should think that Marcus will account for most of those."

"This is getting exciting!" Ken chuckled. "What next?"

Next was a telegraph boy with two telegrams from a shipping company at Southampton. They tore the first open while the boy waited in case there was an answer and made friends with Diccon.

"Please acknowledge giraffes," Merryl read out. "Letter following shortly!" She glanced at the others. "Shipment from Tanagra, in South Africa."

"I believe Lady Morden has a cousin there," Teddy said. "Did it say giraffes—in the plural?" he went on, trying to keep his voice steady. "It might be a printing mistake."

"What's in the other?" Dodie twittered.

Ken seized it. "Ring-tailed lemur and marmosets dispatched on the fifteenth. Letter following!"

"That's from her brother on tour round the world, I should think," Teddy choked. "Great suffering snakes, who's coming now?"

Milly raced off to see.

"The cat's-meat man with requests that we place an order with him weekly for our carnivores!"

"But we've only got one and it isn't eating meat yet—unless"—Merryl paled at the idea—"unless there are some lions and tigers coming and he's in some mysterious way got wind of it. Well, let's take things as they come. Tell him to leave his address, for we'll want him later, and Dodie—oh, Dodie, say no answer to that telegraph boy, and, oh, dear, my head's in a perfect whirl, but—what fun it all is! I think keeping animals is the greatest thrill ever invented."

They ate a hasty lunch and then it was decided that while Ken and Milly kept zoo for the afternoon the others had better go to the station and see if they could get any information about the new arrivals.

It was a pleasant, cool day, with real September sunshine, but the heats of summer were over at last and no one was so very sorry to see them go, for when much work has to be done very hot weather is trying. The lindens, always the last trees to leaf and the first to fall, were turning gold and butter-yellow and showering the hedges with broad heart-shaped leaves. A blue haze brooded on the distance; the woods on the far-off beacon hill were shot with coming russets and wine colours.

Far ahead above the trees, Merryl thought she saw two smokestacks moving along and for a moment wondered what strange car was this a-gipsying along the high road. Then the truth hit her and she clutched Teddy's arm.

"There!" she pointed an excited finger. "The giraffes! They're coming."

"Where? You're joking," he answered, for a bend in the road hid the swaying smokestacks.

Dodie was absolutely simmering over. Another five hundred yards and they rounded a corner to see a remarkable sight.

Two magnificent giraffes were ambling along in the charge of a small band of hired porters. The beasts' gentle, superior faces were full of a mild surprise. Their high sloping shoulders, thick hides, with the rich colouring so well known to every child who has had the supreme joy of a Noah's Ark, the great cloven feet and silly stumpy tails, made such a bizarre picture on that quiet English road that it would not have been surprising to see a great crowd following. But, no, the rural mind about Flaxstead took things with a calm philosophy. When old Gaffer Jones at the 'Dog and Duck' asked 'what war passing out thar?' and begged Granfer Smith to take a peep and see, that fine old fellow returned the answer that it were 'naught but some new animilses for they childer up to Flaxstead'.

The gang joined the porters and turned to go back with them. They found the giraffes' names were Lofty and Lighthouse, and one of the men handed over a quantity of papers with which he had been entrusted regarding the animals' food.

"That's what they 'ad on the boat coming over, the man in charge at the docks told me, and I was to mention that one of them seemed to be unusual skittish, 'e said. But, bless you, miss, they's the best-

tempered critturs ever I see and wouldn't hurt a
fly."

But Merryl felt that it would take a little time to
get used to being looked down upon, for, glancing
up, she caught Lofty's large eye fixed on her,
and she quailed before its magnificent aloofness.
She felt that the giraffes were summing up the
situation quietly and reserving their judgment.
When they reached the zoo the men went back and
left the children in charge.

She took the rope of one beast, while Teddy and
Dodie took the other.

"Come on, let's go right up to camp and surprise
them," she said. "I wonder where they all are?
D'you know, I've the funniest feeling that things
have been happening while we've been away.
There's a sort of—I don't know—left-over excitement in the air."

"Fancy," Dodie said doubtfully. "Here, hold up,
you!" For Lighthouse had shown a desire to double
back in the direction of Bramble Cottage. They got
the giraffes up to the sea-lions' lake and then yelled
for the others. There was a scuffling sound and they
came, flushed with the turmoil of some passing
victory.

"This is Lofty and Lighthouse," Merryl cried
proudly, but Ken and Milly seemed quite unmoved.

"Nice-looking little fellows," Ken said, while
Milly brushed the untidy hair out of her eyes.

"Percy the dingo dog is in the tool-shed, the twelve caballeros are in Dodie's empty tea-chest, and Bernadino is teasing Marcus unmercifully!"

"What—where—how?" Dodie gasped, sitting down weakly on a bucket. "We thought we'd got the cream of the collection."

Merryl and Teddy were laughing helplessly, but Milly and Ken gazed at them with dismay.

"It's no laughing matter," Milly began. "We think we've done marvels of organisation, for there were two crates of oranges as a present from Shipter's Stores, and Toni, the zebra foal, is in the far paddock. He came from someone local."

"What are the others?" Merryl begged. "You know—the caballeros and Bernadino?"

"Oh, they're *adorable*!" Milly squeaked. "Twelve are marmosets; size of squirrels and such woolly fur. Listen; you can hear them in their tea-chest squabbling over some toms we gave them."

A chorus of shrill twittering as of fifty frenzied birds rose stridently.

"Those can't be marmosets," Merryl objected. "They're birds!"

But they opened the tea-chest and confronted her with the twelve lovesome fur cushions set with jewelled pins for eyes. She could only clasp her hands and almost weep for joy at the treasures that were theirs.

"This is Bernadino," Ken said, exhibiting a ring-tailed lemur which had come at the sound of voices, and it was Teddy who lost his head completely now.

"Oh, I *say*!" he exclaimed, holding out his arms, and the friendly little beast ran up him like up a tree to crouch chittering on his shoulder, its handsome ringed tail curled round its own neck for warmth.

The dingo dog and Rupert were disputing a bone near the sea-lions' pond. Dodie, gazing round at the wonderful range of creatures, took a deep breath and voiced everyone's feelings when she said: "Well, it's worth coming a long way to see now. I think it is worth sixpence entrance fee of anyone's money. Oh, and isn't it a wonderful thought that we've done it all ourselves?"

"It's time for the giraffes' supper," Teddy said much later that day. "I've cut them some spiffing fine soft grass, a whole basketful. But how are they to get it?"

The board of directors sallied out to have a look at Lofty and Lighthouse. Feeding time was no light matter these days. Marcus was giving Norah her bottle, Ken was busy with Uff-guff's fishy tea, having taken grapes and tomatoes to the marmosets and Bernadino. The Nubian goat and the Belgian hare were feeding in stodgy content, Diccon was picking over his hay thoughtfully, and all the other creatures were occupied in the same absorbing pastime of stuffing.

The two giraffes saw their supper coming, and they licked their jaws with their long snaky tongues, which in giraffes are some eighteen inches long. They swayed their broad, flat-looking necks and waited in superior calm. One of them kept giving silly little coughs and was trying to rub his neck against a tree.

"Supper, darlings," Merryl called. "Come and get it!"

They came forward slowly with the peculiar rolling gait of their kind and stood towering over the children, gazing down with their huge soft eyes, gazelle-like in their dark beauty, fringed by silky lashes that any film-star might envy. But they did not seem to have much idea of reaching down to eat, though Milly said she remembered pictures of them doing so.

"This won't do," Merryl said decidedly. "Diccon, you come here. I don't see why you shouldn't work just as well as Marcus."

Diccon shambled over to the little group and said *Phrumph*, his little eyes rolling curiously at the giraffes as if to warn them to keep their distance. It must have been a blow to poor Diccon's pride to be told to hoist the basketful of grass to the top of the lean-to and hold it there from slipping while those spotted beauties fed. He pretended not to understand, backing away and grunting, but Merryl had had the great idea that was to make her zoo one of the most famous in all England and she was perfectly ruthless. Years after, animal-lovers came in their hundreds to see the principle of self-help she started really being made to work.

It was Dodie who had the grand idea of a wedding present for Aunt Penny. "Oh *yes*," the others all cried, and Teddy screamed: "Yes, and a guard of honour from the church door exactly like they do at those society weddings in the papers."

"Well, we'll have to talk of it and find a way," said Merryl. "Now, as to this present, it's a bully notion. How much can we all cough up?"

"Not zoo funds!" Milly said decidedly. "This has got to be on our own."

They all agreed. In her quiet way the good little aunt had done so much for them, had worked long hours uncomplainingly making up strange dishes of food for the different animals, walking miles for Uff-guff's fish when the van failed to come, and doing countless other jobs in her long day. They all felt a glow of pleasure to think that it was through the zoo that Aunt Penny had found her happiness. They passed the hat round then and there, and Marcus, coming into the lean-to, could hardly contain his bewildered wonder as to what they were doing. He raised and lowered his jutting brows, wrapped his arms round his body, appearing to be trying to hold in his overwhelming excitement. When they counted the result, he rushed forward to see, peering alternately into the hat and into their faces as if trying to discover whether or no they were pleased.

"Two pounds, five and elevenpence halfpenny," Ken announced. "Funds low—end of holidays. Well, look, we'll give back the odd shillings and pence and just use the two pounds. What shall we get?"

They discussed many things, from a complete set of Dickens to a bead necklace. Finally Dodie said: "How about two of us going up to Flaxstead or even further and finding something really nice in the shops? Better than trying to think!"

This was voted a good idea, and they drew lots, a proceeding which positively convulsed Marcus, and he insisted on drawing too but got a blank. Dodie and Teddy were chosen and they departed forthwith, as there was not much time to lose. The others went to look the animals over for the guard of honour, leaving Marcus solemnly pulling the old hat to pieces as if to see what had been the whole idea of dipping into it.

Certainly Lighthouse was a skittish fellow, for he was executing a dainty dance all by himself on the lawn and galloped away when he saw Merryl coming, moving in a peculiar way, like a nimble rocking-horse.

"I think he'll behave if he doesn't get too restless waiting," Merryl thought, admiring the gentle expression of this sweetest tempered of beasts and marvelling anew at his coloured spots, or, rather, patches, and the strange 'horns' covered by shiny hair, and the funny sloping back, on which it would have been impossible to ride.

When Teddy and Dodie got back it was agreed that they could not have done better. A little travelling-clock in cream enamel was so sweetly right that Milly said almost wistfully that it must be fun getting married and having things given you.

They all wrote on a little card and then wrapped the present up in a great number of papers and coloured string, and Merryl took it to Bramble Cottage to hide until the day. Marcus fingered the paper left lying about, and, as they said afterwards, they ought to have known what would happen. The ape became inflamed by this new joy of wrapping things. This *was* a new game if you like!

Ken first missed Norah's feeding-bottle next morning. "Blowed if I can think where it is," he said. "I always put it back on this shelf!"

"Except when you don't," Dodie said rudely, and later was made to apologise.

Merryl was upset, because feeding-bottles were costly. But it could not be helped; they would have to have one, for though they improvised with an ordinary bottle and a rag teat, Norah did not like it and choked, miserably. Other things disappeared through the morning, and Dodie was at her wits' end to know what to do for the marmosets, for their dish had gone and in it their carefully prepared food for lunch.

"Do you know, I believe Marcus is at the bottom of this," Merryl said. "He's got that expression on his face when he's trying to hide something. Look where he's sitting over there; the very back of his head looks as if he were listening."

They instituted a watch but the ape appeared quite blameless, sunning himself all afternoon and occasionally bursting out into a prolonged chattering of excitement. But at supper-time all was revealed.

Ken had just put out their packets of sandwiches and was making the coffee when Marcus sneaked into the lean-to carrying something carefully. When the gang gathered, he was sitting in a corner hugging himself and rolling his eyes till the whites showed. By each plate was a package very clumsily rolled up in paper.

They were all too stupefied to laugh, and so the poor brute's feelings were spared, for there is something very pathetic in the dim groping copying of man's acts in which the bigger apes indulge.

"Marcus, darling, this is your doing," Merryl cried as she unwrapped her present, to disclose Norah's feeding-bottle. Ken, struggling for composure, undid a log of wood which for two days had been the joy of Marcus's life. Teddy had the marmosets' food-dish, Milly a spoon, and Dodie a coloured pebble which had caught the ape's fancy.

"Come on and be hugged, Marcus," Merryl cried, and Marcus came joyfully, chattering and laughing his ape laugh, which bared his gums, shaking hands with himself in his own peculiar overhead way.

It was a pity, of course, that they praised him so much for his cleverness instead of trying to point out the wickedness of stealing. But as Aunt Penny and Uncle John said afterwards when all was explained, you can't think of everything at once. Marcus indulged in no more presents at meals and for two days life went on perfectly. Then, as if by instinct, Merryl knew that the black imp was up to some tricks again. But though she watched him like a hawk he evaded her and was lost for one whole afternoon, slipping back to his place so quietly that none could have said when he returned. Several more large pieces of paper disappeared, and Merryl groaned.

"He's wrapping things up again," she thought frenziedly. "Come on, Marcus, where have you put what you've stolen this time? Come on, own up!"

But the ape merely rolled on the ground in a transport of joy, kicking his short black legs out and thumping himself in his delight. She tried cuffing him gently, at which his laughs became so up-roarious that she feared he was about to have a fit and left him hurriedly.

But at feeding time next morning the blow fell. She had just tidied up the goat's pen and was carry-ing away the soiled straw when something kicked into one corner caught her eye. She investigated and was completely puzzled. The thing was a sodden-looking lump of something like plum-pudding that had been soaked in water all mixed up with thick white crunchy stuff. Her first awful thought was that someone had been trying to poison the animals; then commonsense prevailed. She found a bit of wrapping paper.

"Dash that ape!" she cried, with as much heat as she ever did show. "What a mercy the goat had too much sense to eat his present, whatever it was! I think I shall have to spank Marcus to break this habit."

She was worried when she found a similar gift by the side of the sea-lions' pond, but Diccon had none, so she concluded he had eaten his, as she found the empty paper.

Her fears mounting, she made a systematic search in the hope of finding a present its owner had not messed up, so that she could identify it. She found what she sought in the giraffes' corner. At her stricken cry the others came at the double. No one had ever seen poor Merryl look like this.

"I could *massacre* Marcus," she sobbed. "Oh, poor Aunt Penny! After all her love and work— to treat her so. Of course, he got it when he was off all that time, sneaked home to Bramble Cottage!"

"Got what?" Dodie cried.

"The cake—the wedding cake. He's been cutting it up and giving pieces all round. The miserable little bounder! All that lovely icing and almond paste, and she was so pleased with it! I daren't go and tell her; it'll kill her!"

"No, it won't," Dodie said seriously, for she had most plain horse-sense of them all. "She's too big to grieve over the loss of something to eat. Come on; let's get it over with; I'll come too."

"We'll all go," they cried, "but we'll spank Marcus first." They knew that if he weren't stopped he'd soon begin stealing from strangers and might have to be shut up. But Marcus, very sore and very warm when they had done with him, could see no sense in it at all. He'd tried to make everyone happy as he saw humans were happy when they got things given and *this* was what happened!

When Aunt Penny heard and understood and went to the larder to see the ruins of her effort, she was shocked. Then her sense of humour came to her rescue. She sat down where she was, the cake on her knee, and began to laugh. She laughed till the tears ran down her face and dropped on to the cracked icing. They stared at her in wonder and huge admiration.

"Oh, chicks, he's only had half!" she said magnificently. "There will be a taste all round. Don't look so woebegone and don't punish him, poor dear. He knew no better!"

"He's *had it*!" Merryl cried almost viciously. "Aunt Penny, you are a brick!"

As they walked home, Dodie said slowly: "We'll make it up to her. That guard of honour shall be perfect if we can do it!"

"They shan't be brought along till the last minute and then they won't get nervous, Lighthouse especially," Milly suggested. "How are you going to get them to cross their necks over the porch?"

"Tie 'em together," Ken said brutally as they reached the zoo, but he was silenced out of hand by Norah coming to look for someone with whom to play. She knocked the boy over, then proceeded to climb all over him and put one fubsy foot on his face, effectually stopping his mouth.

"Thank you, Norah," Teddy said, with unusual venom. "Now, about those necks. What if one of us stood underneath and, at the last minute, threw up something to attract their attention? They'd lean over to look at it and there you are!"

They tried this out on the giraffes, but got poor results and began to be quite worried as to the outcome. So they tried training them like circus horses, running in circles to a rope and being taught right wheel and left wheel, at which they looked simple and foolish. Evidently the giraffes took a dim view of the whole thing.

It was Ken who suggested trying to get them to stand opposite each other and quite simply leave it at that, hoping that they would not shamble off or back away. Because they could think of nothing better the others agreed.

So they practised with the giraffes, getting them to line up and stand opposite one another, and Marcus sat by and watched and hooded his brows in wonder, as if puzzled in his dim brain as to what the humans wanted *now*! He would retire and sit thinking, a sagacious expression on his face, and once Merryl found him leaning two sticks together as if they were the giraffes' necks, and she trembled to think that he had understood their shouts and gestures and the way they'd tried to get the beasts to do their stuff.

The morning of the wedding came. It was to be quiet, for Aunt Penny had only a few real friends instead of, as many people have, a whole lot of acquaintances. She had chosen a pretty dark-blue suit to be married in and carried a bunch of Summerleyton flowers, which the girls had gathered for her. The children slipped out before the ceremony was over, and Ken, who had been well schooled in his part, was on time from the zoo, leading Lofty and Lighthouse.

"Quick! They're nearly through the last hymn," Merryl gasped.

But would those giraffes behave? They were scared; their gentle eyes were round with fear; they shuffled their big cloven feet on the sandy path. Some villagers assembled to see the guests come out did not make matters any better by chattering and laughing and getting in the way. Merryl and Milly were almost in tears, for it had been such a happy plan and they knew that Aunt Penny would have liked it. But it was too late! The march was playing, there was a flash of frocks in the church porch, and those blessed giraffes had just swung completely round and were facing the wrong way!

And then a black streak burst through the crowd, and one woman yelped with terror, thinking she was seeing things. Marcus came charging down the path, his arms above his head as he ran, ape fashion. In his hands he carried a bunch of the sweet grass the giraffes so loved and which they found so difficult to reach even by straddling their long legs apart. Up into the elms Marcus went, chattering to himself, and out along a limb, where he yelled and waved his grass and said '*chee chee!*' Perhaps he was sorry and trying to make amends!

The big animals turned round to look at their zoo companion, and they saw the sweet grass. Face to face as they should be, they reached up to lip it, but the ape screamed with joy at his success and fed them only tufts so that his triumph might be longer-lived. He did not know why they had wanted the beasts just there, but he was gleeful that he had done what they could not do.

When the people streamed out there was a perfect arch above them, and reporters and cameramen alike said it was unique. There was a happy, pleased smile on Mrs. Naylor's face as she saw her favourites so cleverly doing their bit and she never guessed how hard had been the rehearsals.

"Marcus, catch *this*!" Ken whispered wickedly, and tossed up a small bag. The ape in a transport of delight burst it, thinking it contained fruit, and down fluttered a stream of coloured confetti to the cheers of all.

Summerleyton House was got ready and Bramble Cottage shut up while the Naylors were away, but the children were not idle, for in another week, when Aunt Penny was back, school would begin, but they could face the future easily now. Every day or so some parcel of food, some gift of fruit or crate of fish, arrived from admirers, and most of the zoo problems were settled.

Merryl, Dodie, Milly, Ken and Teddy had the zoo a going concern, and their future was rosy with promised joy. On the morning of the Naylors' return they made a special effort. All was tidy as a pin. Each animal had a white bow on neck or tail or a ribbon on its cage. The sea-lions were barking joyfully. The sun shone.

"There they are," Ken cried as steps were heard approaching.

But, no, not this time—only the parcels postman leading a 'parcel' with a ticket round its neck.

Kruger, the kangaroo, paused a moment to take a look at his new home. He appeared pleased.

"And that ain't all," the postman mourned. "There's some of they wallabies coming by this post tomorrow, only this 'ere was all I could manage today!"